D0345100

Danger Zone

"Back!" Joe shouted. "Everybody back!"

"Quick!" Frank added.

Libby, an English volunteer, was a few feet away from Joe. She seemed frozen in place by the sight of the plummeting stone. Joe grabbed her around the waist and pulled her toward the shelter of the nearest house.

The block of stone crashed down on a pile of rubble at the base of the castle wall. The impact sent a cloud of smaller stones and pebbles flying in all directions like buckshot. One grazed Joe's bare arm. When he looked down, he saw a line of red forming against his tan.

Libby was holding her palm against her cheek. Had a rock hit her, too?

"Are you hurt?" Joe asked her.

"I . . . I . . ." Libby stammered. "Up there. I saw him. Or . . . or something. It looked like a puff of smoke, but I knew. It was the spirit of the Sieur! He doesn't want us here. He is saying, 'Leave!' Or he'll drive us away!"

The Hardy Boys Mystery Stories

**Available from MINSTREL Books
and ALADDIN Paperbacks**

THE **HARDY BOYS**®

168
THE CASTLE CONUNDRUM

FRANKLIN W. DIXON

Aladdin Paperbacks

New York London Toronto Sydney Singapore

First Aladdin Paperbacks edition March 2002
First Minstrel edition July 2001

ALADDIN PAPERBACKS
An imprint of Simon & Schuster
Children's Publishing Division
1230 Avenue of the Americas
New York, NY 10020

Printed in the U.S.A.

10 9 8 7 6 5 4 3

ISBN 0-7434-0683-4

Contents

1 A French Adventure

Seventeen-year-old Joe Hardy stared out the window of the train. He turned and trained his blue eyes on his brother, Frank. "Look," he said excitedly. "On that hilltop. It's a ruined castle!"

Frank, eighteen, leaned forward to see past Joe. "Where?" he asked. "All I see is a blur."

"Oh, never mind," Joe said. "It's already out of sight. You've got to be quicker than that. We're going over a hundred and twenty miles an hour."

Frank grinned and settled back in his seat. He and Joe had boarded the superfast train called the TGV in Paris that morning after breakfast. Now, fewer than three hours later, they were already in the south of France.

Frank and Joe had accompanied their father to Europe, where he was attending a conference on enforcing the UN embargo against illegal diamond transportation. Fenton Hardy was a famous private detective who sometimes asked his two sons for help on tough cases. It had been natural for Frank and Joe to start investigating crimes and solving mysteries on their own. Now they, too, had growing reputations as detectives.

"Too bad we couldn't go to the conference with Dad," Frank remarked after a silence. "Some of the top investigators from around the world will be there. I didn't realize diamond smuggling was such a big problem."

When Joe didn't answer, Frank glanced over. Joe was thumbing through their TVI brochure. The initials stood for Teen Village International. A friend of Fenton's had urged Frank and Joe to spend a couple of weeks in the teen program while they were in France. After talking to him and reading the materials from TVI, they had signed up.

On the cover of the brochure, three laughing teens were lifting a large square stone. Behind them, another guy was spreading mortar on the top of a ragged wall.

"I know about pumping iron," Frank cracked. "But pumping rock? That's a new one."

"We're going to have a blast," Joe replied. "It'll be great to meet kids from different countries. And living in a real village from the Middle Ages—how cool is that!"

"We'll see," Frank said, silently wishing he was going with his dad. "Living in an ancient village will be okay. But it sounds like we have to build the village ourselves."

"*Re*-build," Joe corrected. "That's the point. Once the village is finished, it'll become a center for refugee children from all over. We have fun, and we do something worthwhile at the same time."

The rhythm of the train wheels changed. Frank glanced out the window. A few houses, white with red tile roofs, flashed past. Then a thicker cluster of buildings. They must be getting near a town.

From an overhead speaker, a chime sounded. "Avignon," a voice said. Some quick words of French followed. Then Frank heard, "This stop is Avignon. Passengers for Avignon, please prepare to debark."

"That's us," Frank said. "Come on." He stood up and grabbed his backpack. Joe did the same. They joined the line at the rear of the car and caught a glimpse out the window of a wide boulevard choked with traffic. On the other side were the high stone walls of a fortified city. Frank hoped they would have time to explore it.

The train entered a glass-roofed station shed and glided to a stop. The doors hissed open.

On the platform, Frank and Joe stepped out of the

stream of hurrying passengers and paused, looking around.

"What now?" Joe wondered aloud.

"We let them find us," Frank replied with a quick flip of his dark hair. He grinned and added, "And I think they just did."

A guy in faded jeans and a blue T-shirt with big white letters, *TVI*, walked down the platform toward them. He was about six feet tall, Joe's height and an inch shorter than Frank. He had the lithe movements of a soccer player. His blond hair was cut short, and aviator sunglasses hid his eyes. He reached up and took them off. He was a little older than Frank had first guessed, probably in his late twenties.

"Joe? Frank?" he asked. "I'm Kevin Pierce, from TVI. Welcome to Provence. I've got a car outside."

Frank and Joe shook Kevin's hand. They followed him down some steps and through a tunnel to the station entrance.

"You're American, aren't you?" Joe asked as they crossed a crowded parking lot.

Kevin smiled. "Half," he replied. "My dad is. He was in the Air Force, but he retired a few years ago. My mom is French."

"Where did you grow up? In Europe?" Frank asked.

"Mostly," Kevin said. "But I attended American schools a lot of the time. And I went back to the States for college. Here we are."

4

He pointed to a blue minivan with *TVI* painted on the door. The van's lights flashed briefly, and the side door slid open. Frank realized that Kevin had a remote control in his hand. The Hardys slung their packs in the back. Frank took the front passenger seat. Joe sat behind him.

"Pretty cool," Joe remarked, pointing to the two tinted moonroofs. One was over the front seat and the other over the back.

"Pretty hot, you mean," Kevin retorted. "It gets to be over thirty-five degrees most afternoons. That's the high nineties in Fahrenheit. And it's usually sunny. We're lucky to have A/C in the van. Most people around here don't—it uses too much gas."

He backed out of the slot and joined a line of cars waiting to leave the parking lot. Soon they were driving along the boulevard that followed the city wall. It led them onto a highway lined with furniture shops, tire dealers, gas stations, and fast-food restaurants with familiar names.

"We could almost be back home," Frank said. "This looks like the outskirts of Bayport—except for the French words on the signs."

"Don't worry," Kevin replied. "Pretty soon you'll know you're not in the US anymore. Did anyone brief you on the program, by the way?"

"Not really," Joe said. "We just know what we read in your brochures."

Kevin nodded. "Then you've got the basic concept.

Teenagers from all over the world come to Fréhel to work on restoring the village. Some, like you, come for a week or two. Others stay for one or two months or even longer."

"What about you?" Frank asked. "How long have you been there?"

For a moment Kevin looked blank. Then he laughed. "I'm not a volunteer," he said. "I work for the organization. I'm the assistant to Sophie Parmentier, the director. Not only that, I live in Fréhel. Well, sort of."

"What do you mean?" Joe asked.

"It's a weird coincidence," Kevin said. "My mother's family actually came from Fréhel. They left over a hundred years ago, but they never forgot."

"That's amazing," Frank said.

"Well, the connection was one reason I took the job," Kevin explained. "And a few months ago I bought the cottage my great-grandparents used to live in. It had been empty for years and wasn't much more than a pile of stones. Now I help reconstruct the village during the day, and evenings and weekends I work on my own house."

"Cool," Joe said. "I don't even *know* the house where our great-grandparents lived."

"Are you planning to live there full-time, once the house is done?" Frank asked.

"I hope so," Kevin said. "It all depends. If TVI pulls through, and if they want me to stay on, I'd love

6

to. If not . . . well, I can always get a job in the city and spend vacations there."

"You make it sound as if the program's in trouble," Frank observed. "What's the problem?"

Kevin glanced over at him for a moment. Then he turned his attention back to the road. "Say, you'd make a good detective," he said in a teasing voice.

"As a matter of fact . . ." Joe began to say.

Frank turned and shot Joe a warning glance. He wanted the kids at TVI to treat them as regular members, not as celebrity detectives. Joe bit off the rest of his sentence.

Kevin didn't seem to notice. "It's the usual problem," he continued. "Money. TVI's a nonprofit organization. Sophie spends half her time going around plugging the program and begging for contributions. Our volunteers mostly pay their own way, so we're okay for now. But once we start welcoming refugees, it'll be different. We'll need lots of money."

"Pretty tough," Frank said.

Kevin nodded. "Believe it. Still, you fellows don't have to worry about all that. Just work hard, have fun, and make friends. Oh, and always wear a hat outside. The Provençal sun can be brutal."

Frank could see what he meant. Even through the van's tinted glass, the bright sunlight made him squint. They were out in the countryside now. Fields lined both sides of the two-lane highway. Off to the

7

right, in the distance, a rocky ridge rose steeply from the plain.

"How long a trip is it?" Joe asked.

"About an hour and a half," Kevin told him.

"It was nice of you to meet us at the train," Joe said.

"No problem," Kevin said. "You'd have had a hard time getting to Fréhel if I hadn't. Besides, I did a few errands while I was in Avignon."

Frank looked at the plants in the nearest field. "Are those melons?" he asked.

"You better believe it," Kevin replied. "The melons from around here are the best in the world. The inside's like cantaloupe, but the skin is smooth with green and white stripes. You'll get to try them at breakfast tomorrow. The day after, too. Well, actually, every day."

A few moments later they passed a truck parked on the side of the road. The back was heaped high with green and white melons. A hand printed cardboard sign read, "Melons—5/10F."

"Hey, I can read French!" Joe joked. "Melons, five of them for ten. But what's the *F?*"

"It stands for 'francs,'" Frank told him. "Didn't you know? The French named their money after me!"

Joe leaned forward to punch his shoulder. Frank grinned and dodged the blow.

"Take a look up on the left," Kevin said. "Through the trees on the hillside. See where I mean?"

Frank looked. At first he saw only a steep slope with dusty trees that looked ready to tumble down into the valley. Then his eye picked out a jumble of regular shapes the same color as the rocks. "Is that a town?" he asked.

"More like a village," Kevin replied. "Maybe thirty houses and a church. It's pretty typical of this area. People farmed their fields down in the valley. Come nightfall, though, they went up into the hills to be safe."

"That's not Fréhel, is it?" Joe asked.

"No, we're still twenty kilometers away," Kevin told him. "About twelve miles. But you'll see. Fréhel's built on the same pattern, except there's a castle, too."

The first notes of "Frère Jacques" sounded, then repeated. Kevin pulled a cell phone from his belt and glanced at the display. "Wrong number," he grunted, and put it back.

Frank sat back and gazed out the window. He let the strangeness of the setting sink in. It wasn't any single detail that did it. It was *everything:* the cars, the houses, the plants along the roadside, the shape of the landscape, even the way the center line on the highway was painted. Their day in Paris and the trip on the TGV had been exciting, sure. But now he was really starting to feel that he was in a foreign country. . . .

"Frank?" Joe was shaking his arm. "Frank, wake up. We're almost there."

Frank blinked. His neck and shoulders felt stiff. "Sorry," he murmured. "Jet lag, I guess."

"No problem," Kevin assured him. "That's Fréhel up ahead, on the left."

It was hard to make out against the backdrop of a long, steep ridge. A rocky spur jutted out into the valley, twice the height of a tall building. At the very top, the rocky cliffs merged into the massive stone walls of a ruined castle.

"You can't see the village from here," Kevin continued. He slowed and turned off the highway on to a narrow lane. "It's on the slope behind the castle."

The lane started to climb and wind around a hill. The pavement ended suddenly, and the van did a little sideways slide on the loose dirt and gravel. Kevin muttered and swerved to dodge a pothole. "I wish we had the money to fix this road," he said.

Frank wished so, too. On his side, the van was only inches from the edge of a thirty-foot drop. And, of course, a little back road like this one didn't rate a guardrail, just a few skimpy bushes.

As they rounded a curve, something caught Frank's eye. A tree branch stuck up out of the grass beside the road. Someone must have put it there on purpose. The thick end of the branch was at the top. As they drew near, Frank had the impression that something almost too faint to see stretched from the branch across the road in front of them.

Then they were past. Frank was about to look back when he sensed a movement ahead and to the left. He stared. A big rock had started to roll down the steep hillside toward the road. It was going to crash into the side of the van!

2 Up at the Castle

"Kevin, look out!" Frank shouted. He pointed at the falling boulder. "Stop!"

Kevin held tight to the wheel and slammed on the brakes. The van bucked and began to skid sideways, toward the edge of the drop. Frank grabbed the door handle and braced his feet against the firewall.

As suddenly as it had started, the crisis ended. The van came to a stop in a thick cloud of yellow dust. Through it, Frank saw the big rock rumble across the lane and disappear over the cliff. A moment later a clatter from below told him it had landed at the bottom.

"Whew!" Joe said from the backseat. "That was close. Do you have a lot of falling rocks in this area?"

Kevin backed up a few feet and straightened out.

"Let's put it this way," he said. "At TVI, our unofficial motto is Expect the unexpected. Why did that stone decide to start down the hill just then? No reason . . . but strange things happen around here. You'll get used to it."

Frank opened his mouth to mention the stick he had seen. Then he decided to hold off. This was a new place with a new bunch of people. He wanted to get a sense of it and them before he started making waves.

"I should warn you guys about one thing," Kevin added as he set the van into motion again. "Whatever you see, whatever you hear, whatever the other kids try to tell you, keep this in mind—the chateau of Fréhel is *not* haunted."

"Does that mean some people think it is?" Joe asked.

A muscle in Kevin's cheek twitched. "It's not," he repeated in a louder voice. "It's all a lot of nonsense. Pay no attention, you hear?"

They rounded a curve. The lane became a pair of rutted tracks with a line of thirsty-looking blades of grass growing between them. After a few dozen yards, the track ended at a flat, dusty field. A few vehicles were parked on the far side. They included a couple of cars, a battered motorcycle, and a small truck that looked as if someone had built it out of corrugated roofing. Beyond, a steep path snaked up the rugged slope to the clustered houses and the castle.

Kevin pulled up next to the truck and stopped.

"What is that contraption?" Joe asked, pointing to the truck.

Kevin grinned. "You are looking at a vintage Citroën *camionnette*," he said. "It's a collectors' item. Top speed about forty miles an hour, with a tailwind. But it gets you where you're going."

They got out and Frank and Joe grabbed their backpacks. Kevin swung open the rear door of the van. "You want to give me a hand?" he asked, pointing to the cardboard boxes on the floor.

"Sure," Frank replied. He got a grip on the nearest carton. It was heavy.

Kevin grabbed another carton. "Follow me."

Frank glanced at Joe. Then he gave a meaningful look at the steep climb to the village. They were already carrying loaded backpacks. Was this some kind of test? Well, if so, they were not going to wimp out on their first day!

Joe took a box and followed after Kevin and Frank, who had stopped next to a wheeled platform about three feet square. A metal rail ran straight up the hillside toward the village.

"We're not totally primitive here," Kevin said, smiling. "This lift is our lifeline. If we had to carry all our supplies up the hill on foot, who'd have energy left for our real work?"

Kevin set his carton on the platform. Frank and Joe did the same. "Can it handle our packs, too?" Joe asked.

"Sure," Kevin replied. "Put 'em on." He bent down, opened the door of a control panel, and flipped a switch. The platform moved silently up the hill. Frank noticed a counterweight gliding down the hill at the same pace. He realized they must be linked by a cable.

"Neat," Frank said.

"Designed and built by our TVI members," Kevin told him. "The motor is up at the top. It runs off a solar panel. One thing we have plenty of around here is sunlight!"

Kevin started up the path. Frank touched Joe's arm and motioned with his head for them to fall back a little. In an undertone, he told Joe about the suspicious stick and his impression that there had been something stretched across the lane.

"You mean, right before that rock almost hit us?" Joe demanded. "A booby trap!"

"It wouldn't surprise me," Frank said. "I'd like a look around where it happened. I wonder how we can manage that."

By now Kevin was well ahead of them. He glanced back, as if wondering what was holding them up. Frank and Joe started walking faster. The higher they went, the more the view opened up. Frank could see the whole width of the valley and much of its length. To the right, in the distance, a sizable town spread across the valley floor. Nearer at hand, a humpback stone bridge crossed a dry streambed.

At the edge of the village the path became a narrow street paved with rounded stones set into the ground. A few of the houses were almost intact, but most were in ruins. Openings gaped where windows had been. Walls leaned out toward the street. Sky gleamed brightly through holes in the upper floors and roofs.

Joe looked around and shook his head. "It might be easier to tear this place down and start over!"

Kevin led them to a complete house with urns of flowers on each side of a freshly painted blue door. A rack outside held four or five mountain bikes. He pushed the door open and called, "Sophie? I'm back. I've got our new recruits with me."

They went inside. The room was furnished as an office, with two computers, a laser printer, a scanner, and a fax. A woman in her thirties with short black hair stood up and came over to them.

"How do you do," she said, shaking hands. Her English had a slight accent. "Welcome to Fréhel and TVI. Your roommates are supposed to be here to meet you and show you around. Ah, here they are."

Two guys rushed in and apologized to Sophie for being late. Frank looked them over. They were dressed similarly in khaki shorts and T-shirts with the sleeves cut off. Otherwise, they could not have looked more different. One was slim, with carroty hair, a crop of freckles on his sunburned face and arms, and a Hispanic accent. The other, with the height and heft of an

NFL linebacker, looked African and sounded English.

The redhead turned to Frank and Joe. "Hi," he said. "I am Luis O'Gorman, from Buenos Aires. And this is Welly Freeman, from Pretoria, South Africa. You are Joe and Frank, I know, but which is which?"

"I'm Joe," Joe said. "The handsome blond one."

"Which must mean I'm the brown-eyed smart one," Frank retorted.

They shook hands all around.

"Some of the others are still finishing lunch," Welly said. "Are you fellows hungry?"

"We had something on the train," Joe replied.

"But that was a while ago," Frank quickly added.

"And a while to go until supper," Welly said with a smile. "No restaurants in Fréhel, you know. Come. We'll introduce you round and see what's left to eat."

Frank and Joe thanked Kevin and went with the two guys. As they left the office, Joe pointed to the rack of bikes. "Do you guys ride a lot?" he asked.

"Some," Welly said. "There are nice trails along the ridge, not too challenging. The bikes belong to different people, but they're usually good about lending them."

They walked up the main street, and Frank gestured at the ruined houses on both sides. "How does a town get to be in such terrible shape?" he asked.

"Everyone left," Luis told him. "Some moved to the valley. They wanted to be closer to their fields. The rest just left . . . and never returned."

Frank could tell there was more to the story. What was Luis not saying? And *why* was he holding back?

They came to a cobblestone square, where fifteen or twenty wire folding chairs were scattered in clumps. Along the edge of the square, some scraggly trees fought to survive. On the far side was a stone building that stood taller than the others. Its red tile roof looked new. So did the bright blue shutters framing its tall windows.

"This is our community center," Welly said proudly. "In the old days it was the village school. I painted the shutters myself. I was bright blue for many days afterward."

Frank and Joe followed their guides inside. There were two big rooms. The first was furnished with a battered couch, some folding chairs, and a couple of old desks. A boom box shared the top of a bookcase with a stack of CDs. Luis led them through to the back room.

A rugged wooden farmhouse table stretched the length of the room. The half-dozen people seated around it all turned to look at the Hardys. Welly introduced Joe and Frank, then said, "This is Gert Holst, Siri Banaraike, Jean-Claude de Fréhel, Marie-Laure de Fréhel, Libby Fotheringhay—"

"Hold on!" Frank protested with a laugh. "We can't learn everyone's name at once!"

A girl with light brown hair pulled back in a pony-tail said, "No one expects you to. Here, sit down.

Would you like some bread and cheese? It is a local goat cheese, very good."

Frank took the chair next to her. Joe found a place on the other side of the table.

"Let's see," Frank said, after a bite of bread and cheese. "You are . . ."

"My name is Marie-Laure," she replied. "I'm afraid you Americans find it hard to say."

Frank leaned forward and spoke to the guy on the other side of her. "And you're Jean-Claude, right? Are you two related?"

Marie-Laure smiled. "We are twins. Yet we do not look at all alike! Isn't that strange?"

The guy next to Joe, with a square face and a blond crew cut, said, "You are speaking with our local celebrities. In fact, the village is called after them."

Frank gave Marie-Laure a questioning look. Her cheeks turned pink.

"What Gert means," she said, "is that the chateau and village of Fréhel have been in our family for a long time. Hundreds of years, in fact."

"You mean this village belongs to you?" Joe asked. "I don't get it. What about TVI?"

Jean-Claude said, "Our father was a founder of TVI. He rents the village to the organization for a token sum."

"Imagine being rich enough to own a whole town," Siri said dreamily. "*And* a castle!"

"You don't understand," Marie-Laure said. "We are

19

not rich. We are poor. We cannot afford to pay the taxes on the chateau and the village. And now the government is considering if we must restore the chateau as a historic monument. Everything we have would not be even a fraction of what it would cost to do that!"

"What will you do if that happens?" Frank asked.

Marie-Laure shrugged. "If TVI can raise enough money, maybe we will turn everything over to the group. If not . . . there are developers who would like to buy the town and chateau. They would make this a fancy resort for rich people, not a haven for refugee children. A very great shame, but what can we do? If only we still had our ancestor's treasure . . ."

Gert gave a mocking laugh. "That is no problem," he jeered. "All you must do is ask the old guy where it is. Will he not tell you?"

In a steely voice, Jean-Claude said, "I do not find this funny."

Gert laughed again. "No? But we do. These tales of old spooks howling in the wind and rattling the shutters . . . they are jokes. They are meant to draw tourists. The village is talked of in the press, the TV crews arrive, and *hoopla!* The family will sell the castle and town for a fortune. This, after we sweat to rebuild it for nothing."

Jean-Claude's face turned bright red. "You . . . you . . ." he sputtered. He grabbed a full glass of water off the table. He drew his arm back to fling the water in Gert's face.

3 All Wet

"Jean-Claude!" Marie-Laure exclaimed. *"Non!"* She grabbed her brother's wrist.

Jean-Claude's hand was already in motion. All Marie-Laure did was throw his aim off.

The water in the glass flew across the table, straight at Joe. He saw it coming but too late to duck. He barely had time to scrunch his eyes shut. Then he was instantly soaked, from the top of his head to the middle of his chest.

Joe let out a gasp. The water was chilled. It felt even colder because the day was so warm. Still, he thought, it could have been worse. At least there hadn't been ice cubes in the glass.

Someone put a dry napkin in his hand. He wiped his eyes, then the rest of his face. Across the table,

Frank and the French twins had jumped up from their seats. They were watching him with concern.

"Hey, Joe, are you okay?" Frank demanded.

Joe grinned. "I don't think I've started to melt yet," he replied.

"I am so, so sorry, Joe," Jean-Claude said in an anguished voice. "I am an idiot!"

"You won't get any argument from me," Joe said grimly. He knew the French kid hadn't meant to splash him, and he certainly didn't intend to hold a grudge. Still, Jean-Claude should learn to control his temper. What had Gert said to set him off like that?

"Excuse me," Joe said, pushing himself up from the table. "I'd better go dry off and change shirts."

"I'll show you and Frank where you'll be bunking," Welly offered. "It's right up the hill."

Jean-Claude looked as if he wanted to apologize more. His sister seemed torn between anger and worry. Joe gave them both a brief, meaningless smile and went to find his pack. He and Frank followed Welly onto the street.

"A lot of the village houses just have two floors, with one room on each floor," Welly explained as they walked. "Downstairs was for cooking and eating and living. The whole family slept upstairs. What we're doing is making them over into miniature dormitories, with two bunk rooms. Here, this is us."

The house he pointed to was the last one on the block. The shutters and the door were bright blue.

"Let me guess," Joe said. "You painted them."

Welly's smile flashed. "Right you are! Come, we have the upstairs room. That's lucky. It's at least a degree or two cooler at night."

They went inside and climbed a narrow stone stairway to the upper floor. The room was bigger than Joe expected, with windows on two sides. One of the windows looked directly out at the ruins of the chateau. The furniture consisted of two sets of bunk beds, two dressers, a rickety table, and four wooden chairs.

"It's very basic," Welly said. "But we cope. Luis and I took the bunks and chest near the front window. You fellows get the others."

Joe and Frank did a quick round of scissors-paper-stone. Frank won and chose the top bunk. Joe slung his pack on the bottom bunk, opened it, and rooted around for a dry shirt and a towel. Then he stripped off his sodden T-shirt, rubbed down, and pulled the clean shirt on.

"Now what?" he asked Welly as he combed his hair with his fingers. "What's the program?"

"Midafternoon is free time," Welly replied. "It's too hot to work outside in the sun. Some of the kids even take siestas. But starting at four, we put in another couple of hours before supper. There's usually some sort of evening activity as well. The schedule is posted on the bulletin boards at the office and the community center."

Frank glanced at his watch. "So we're on our own for the next hour or so? Maybe we'll just walk around and get to know the place."

"All right," Welly said. "But take a water bottle and wear a hat. It gets fierce out there. And if you go into rocky areas, watch yourself. We see *vipères* now and again—poisonous snakes."

"What do they look like?" Joe asked.

"Tan with brown spots, and about so long," Welly told him. He held his hands a foot and a half apart. "Not very big as snakes go, but rather deadly even so."

"We'll be on the lookout," Joe promised.

When Welly had left, Frank said, "Let's go look at the place where that rock fell."

"Just what I was going to suggest," Joe replied. He grabbed a baseball cap from his pack and a half-empty water bottle from the side pocket. "We can stop by the dining room and refill this."

The dining room was empty. In the kitchen, two middle-aged women in aprons were cleaning up. They spoke no English but understood when Joe held up his water bottle. Soon the Hardys were on their way again. They retraced their steps through the village and down to the parking lot. A ten-minute walk brought them to the area of the near accident.

"Here's where the rock fell," Joe said. He pointed to traces on the roadside. "It must be one of those down below."

"And that stick I saw was about thirty feet farther

down the road," Frank said. He paced along, studying the grass and bushes that edged the narrow track. Suddenly he stopped and bent down.

"Ha!" Frank said, straightening up. He held a yard-long branch in his hand. Joe drew closer. "And look at this!"

A length of clear nylon fishing line was tied around one end of the branch.

"So it *was* a booby trap!" Joe said. "Let's see if we can find the rest of it."

That turned out to be harder. They scrambled up the hill, watching for small tan snakes as well as fishing line. After ten minutes of sweaty, dusty searching, Joe was ready to quit when he spotted a coil of line under a bush. They followed it along the hillside. At the far end they found it tied to a short, thick piece of wood.

"Check me on this," Joe said. "You take a big rock and prop it in place with the wood. Then you run the line along and across the road. A car hits the line, it jerks out the prop, and the rock starts rolling downhill."

"Sounds good to me," Frank said. "The question is, did whoever set the trap know who would spring it? Or didn't he care?"

"I think he knew," Joe replied. "Look—this is meant for somebody coming *up* the road. If somebody leaving the village sprang it, they'd be long gone before the rock hit the road."

Frank nodded. "Good point, Joe. In other words, it was probably aimed at Kevin . . . or at you and me."

"No way!" Joe protested. "I don't expect everybody to like us. But if they're going to roll big rocks at us, couldn't they at least wait until after they *meet* us?"

The work site that afternoon was a house that was little more than a roofless shell. One wall had collapsed into a heap of stones. Kevin put Joe and Frank to work sorting the loose stones. They were to put those with one flat side on the left and those with two on the right. Those with three or more—a precious few— they carried to a special pile near the old fireplace.

A Belgian boy named Manu helped the Hardys get the hang of the job. "The ones with no flatness, just roll behind you," he said. "Only lift the good ones. Or else it is way too much work."

After the first half hour, Joe was ready to say it was way too much work, period. His back and shoulders ached from all the lifting. He was wearing thick leather work gloves, but even so his hands felt raw. And the shirt he was wearing was as soaked as the last one but not with ice water.

At five o'clock everyone took a break. Joe found a shady spot and threw himself on the ground. Welly sat down next to him. "Don't worry," he said. "We all felt that way our first day."

"Why couldn't these dudes build their houses out of wood?" Joe groused. "Or at least use smaller rocks!"

"Wood was too scarce," Welly replied. "And with big stones, the walls go up faster. You'll see. In a day or two, you'll get to do some stone laying. We all trade off jobs, you know. That makes it more interesting."

"I hope *something* does," Joe groaned. "My arms are turning to stone and my mind is turning to mush."

The next hour went faster and was easier. When Joe found a stone that was flat on all six sides, he almost let out a cheer. And when Kevin rang a bell to end the work period, he saw that the big heap of stones was practically gone. He looked over at Frank, and they exchanged grins.

Next came showers in a roofless enclosure. It reminded Joe of the changing room at the beach back home. He and Frank had just finished dressing when the dinner bell rang.

The Hardys were among the last to enter the dining room. They paused at the door and looked around. Marie-Laure waved and pointed to two seats between her and her brother. Joe was torn. He might have liked to sit with some of the people he hadn't met yet. However, saving the seats was the French girl's way of making up for that glass of water in the face. It would be rude of him to refuse it.

The meal started with pâté and thick slices of crusty country bread. Next was chicken stewed with carrots and onions. After platters of sliced tomatoes with basil leaves and olive oil came warm homemade apple tart and an assortment of cheeses.

"Do you eat like this all the time?" Frank asked Jean-Claude.

Jean-Claude raised his eyebrows and shrugged his shoulders. "Sometimes for an event we have a special meal," he replied.

Joe caught Frank's eye and smiled. *This* meal seemed pretty special to him!

"We have a custom here," Marie-Laure said. "After dinner we go up to a ledge near the chateau to watch the sunset. It is a way of being more together."

"Sounds nice," Joe said. "But tell me something. You keep calling the castle a chateau. I thought a chateau was like a palace, with fountains and gardens and stuff."

"Sometimes it is," Marie-Laure explained. "But Fréhel is what we call a *château fort,* a strong chateau. Those others came later, when the need for high walls was less."

Welly, across the table, added, "We get the word *castle* from French. So it's really the same thing."

On the way to the ledge, the Hardys walked with Luis, Welly, and Gert. As they passed the entrance to the castle, Gert said, "Watch out, guys. You don't want the Sieur to get you."

"What does that mean?" Frank asked.

"It's a local legend," Luis said. "The Sieur de Fréhel was a nobleman. He explored the world—

Africa, Asia, South America . . . When he returned, he brought back a fabulous treasure in diamonds."

"Sounds like the Count of Monte Cristo," Frank said.

"Sort of," Welly said. "But this guy was for real. He was the ancestor of the twins, in fact."

"So this is the lost treasure Marie-Laure mentioned this afternoon?" Joe asked. "What happened to it?"

"That is a long story," Luis said. "It can wait."

They scrambled up a rocky path to the ledge. The view was terrific. So was the drop from the front edge. As the sun moved closer to the horizon, it became huge and dark orange.

"Wow!" Joe said. "That is really spectacular!"

Gert gave a sour smile. "Yes. The cause is air pollution from power plants along the Rhone River."

"This guy's a load of laughs," Joe muttered to Frank.

Soon the sun was down. The landscape darkened in the valley below, but the sky stayed a brilliant light blue.

The teens started back to the village. Frank turned to Luis. "What about that long story?"

"Ah," Luis said. "Yes. This was in the days of Napoleon. After his fall, there was a lot of unrest. Some former soldiers turned bandit. A bandit gang heard of the hoard of jewels at Fréhel. They attacked the chateau. The Sieur and his men held them off while his wife and children escaped through a secret tunnel, but the bandits were too many."

"What happened then?" Joe asked, wide-eyed.

Welly took up the story. "The diamonds were in a secret hiding place. The Sieur wouldn't tell the gang where. They tried to torture him, but he died of a heart attack. The bandits were furious. They took his body up to the highest wall and threw it over."

"Wait a minute," Frank said. "How do we know all this?"

"The Sieur's wife spread the alarm," Luis told him. "Mounted troopers came from the nearest town. They captured some of the bandits, who confessed before they were executed."

"And the treasure was never found?" Joe asked.

"No," Welly said. "Not only that—the Sieur's body was never found either. The local peasants said he still prowled the chateau and the village. Later, some treasure seekers were found at the bottom of the wall with their necks broken."

"This is why the village became deserted," Luis added. "The people were scared away."

"That is quite a story," Frank said.

"It is not yet over," Gert told him. "There is reason to think the Sieur still roams his domain. If so, he cannot be happy to see all these intruders. Do not be surprised if one of *us* is found with a broken neck!"

4 Lost in the Maze

Gert's prediction of danger seemed to hang over the group like a threatening cloud. Frank glanced at Welly and Luis. Their faces were carefully blank. Did they really take this ghost story seriously?

Back at the square, some of the kids went inside to listen to music. Most stayed outside to talk and enjoy the night air. As the newest arrivals, Frank and Joe were the center of interest. Everyone wanted to get to know them.

Quite a few wanted to talk about the USA, too. Whatever country they were from, they knew the names and histories of American pop groups and movie stars. They watched American TV shows, wore American jeans and sneakers, and ate American burgers. What they got from all this, though, was a little peculiar.

"No," Frank heard Joe telling a Spanish girl. "We don't really have a gang problem at Bayport High School. And nobody I know brings a gun to class."

A guy named Narguib, from Alexandria, Egypt, asked Frank about the personal life of his favorite rap artist. "Is he really as wild as they say?"

"Beats me," Frank said. "I've heard of him, but that's about it."

"How can that be?" Narguib demanded. "Didn't you say you live in New York? So does he!"

Frank started to explain the difference between New York City and New York State. Narguib wasn't interested. He obviously thought Frank was holding out on him.

Marina was different. She was from one of the Greek islands. Her aunt and uncle lived in a town not far from Bayport. She had visited them a year earlier and wanted to talk about places she remembered.

"We went to a wonderful restaurant for fish," she said. "It was built out over the water. From outside it looked like nothing, but inside it was very elegant."

"I think I know the place," Frank said. "It's in Herrick's Cove, and it's got a French name."

"That's right," Marina exclaimed. "I remember now—Au Vieux Port. What a small world this is!"

The light faded slowly. As the darkness grew, Frank noticed the others drifting off. Luis and Welly came over. "We are going back to the room now," Luis announced. "The sun comes up very early."

Frank looked at his watch. To his surprise, it was already after ten. He held back a yawn. "Good idea," he said. "It's been a long day."

The blackness that surrounded Frank was total. He held his breath and listened. Something told him he was in the center of a huge space—a sports arena, perhaps, or an airplane hangar. From nearby came a scribbly sound like plastic scraping on stone. It was followed by a tiny squeal so high pitched that he wasn't sure he'd heard it at all. He wanted to move away from it, but he didn't dare. For all he could tell, he might be standing at the edge of a dangerous drop.

A pale glow filled the air. It came from inside the rough stones that he now saw walled him in. He was at the bottom of a deep, narrow shaft. Metal rungs led up one side, but when he touched one it burned his hand. The squealing was louder now. He glanced down and gasped. He was standing in the middle of hundreds of squirming rats. They stared at him with bloodred eyes and bared their sharp white teeth. The braver ones started to climb up his legs. He stamped his feet to shake them loose.

There was a low opening in one of the walls of the shaft. Why hadn't he noticed it before? He ducked through and found himself in a long, curving corridor. At the far end, someone was just vanishing around the bend. Maybe it was someone who knew how to get out of here. Frank set off at a run. Soon the other guy was in sight again.

"Hey!" Frank called. "Hey, wait up!"

The words bounced around the stone corridor like a thunderclap. The stranger didn't turn. Frank ran faster. He was starting to think that he had seen the guy before somewhere. He had narrowed the gap to less than twenty feet when he remembered where. It was in the three-way mirror of a clothing store. He was looking at his own back.

Suddenly the other figure stopped walking and began to turn around. . . .

Frank sat up suddenly. He was breathing quickly, and his forehead was damp. Some dream! It still felt real. He turned his head. The room was dark, but the windows were paler from the sky's glow. He slid to the end of the bunk and climbed down the crossbars to the floor. The tiles were cool on his bare feet.

His lips and tongue felt dry. He remembered that Joe had left the water bottle on the dresser. He groped his way over, waving his hands in front of him to keep from bumping into anything.

As he passed the window that looked out on the chateau, he paused. Bluish white beams from the rising moon lit the front of the ruins and cast the rest in deeper darkness. Frank wished he had his camera with him. Not that film could really capture such a magical scene.

Suddenly he held his breath and stared. A light had just appeared at one of the openings in the chateau's wall. He knew it wasn't reflected moonlight. The color was all wrong, a sickly green like rotting wood. There it was again, at a different window.

Frank tiptoed over to the bunk and felt for Joe's shoulder. Joe sat up.

"Wha—" he muttered drowsily.

"Quick, come over to the window," Frank whispered. "I want you to see this."

It took Joe a moment to understand. By the time they made it to the window, the strange glow was gone.

"You were dreaming," Joe murmured.

"No, that was before," Frank replied. "This was real. I saw it."

"Yeah, right," Joe said. He started back toward his bunk. "That's what you get for listening to ghost stories right before bedtime."

In the morning Frank awoke before the sun rose. The sky was still pale gray. When he climbed down from his bunk, the shaking of the bed woke Joe as well. In whispers, Frank suggested they take a walk before the others got up.

The hillside was loud with birdsong. A cool breeze rustled the herbs that grew wild all around. Once they were away from the village, Frank said,

"There's something going on here. Something that's not right. I think we should try to get to the bottom of it."

"You mean that booby trap yesterday?" Joe asked.

"That, sure," Frank replied. "Plus whoever was sneaking around the chateau during the night. And beyond that, there's a funny atmosphere. Something doesn't feel right."

"Maybe it's just somebody's idea of a joke," Joe suggested. "Somebody like Gert, for instance. I can imagine him pulling stunts to make people believe the chateau is haunted."

"Not very funny," Frank pointed out. "If that rock had hit the car, Kevin might have gone right over the side. Luckily he stopped in plenty of time."

"Okay, but what exactly are we looking for?" Joe asked.

Frank pounded his fist into his palm. "I wish I knew," he said. "At this point all we can do is talk to lots of people and keep our eyes and ears open. I hope we're imagining things. But I don't think so."

They got back to the village just as the bell rang for breakfast. The long table was set with pitchers of coffee and hot milk, baskets of bread, and dishes of different flavors of jam. Frank took a seat next to the English girl, Libby. Joe sat farther down the table, between Gert and Siri.

Frank picked up the nearest pitcher of coffee. It smelled wonderful. He looked for a cup or mug,

36

but there wasn't one. The only crockery at each place was a small plate and an upside-down cereal bowl.

Libby noticed his confusion and giggled. "It's a French custom," she explained. "At breakfast, you drink café au lait in what they call a *bol*, pronounced 'bowl.' Oh, and you're supposed to pour the coffee and hot milk at the same time, from opposite sides of the bowl. Here, like this."

She turned his bowl right side up, took the two pitchers, and poured. The hot milk foamed up and left a thin layer of bubbles on the surface of the coffee.

"Thanks," Frank said. He picked up the bowl of coffee and took a sip. It was delicious, but the sides of the bowl burned his fingers. "Anything else I need to know at this point?"

"Well . . . you needn't expect a decent breakfast while you're here," Libby said. "Bread, butter, and jam, that's it. They do sell cereal in the stores, but the French mostly think it's a foreign fad. As for a really bang-up meal of eggs, a rasher of bacon, fried tomatoes, and toast, no such luck!"

"How do you like TVI?" Frank asked. "Aside from the breakfast menu?"

"It was really super at first," Libby replied. "But now I'm wondering if I should finish out the time I signed on for. I don't like all this ghost business. It makes me very uneasy."

"The story about the Sieur de Fréhel, you mean?" Frank probed.

"Not exactly," Libby said. "A story's just a story. I don't avoid the East End of London because of tales about Jack the Ripper. No, it's little things. Noises at night. Glimmers of light where no one ought to be. A tool that isn't where you put it down just a moment before. I daresay you think this all sounds remarkably silly."

"No, I don't," Frank assured her. "But Joe and I just got here yesterday afternoon. I haven't had time to notice much. I'd like to hear more about your experiences."

Before Libby could reply, Kevin, at the end of the table, stood up and tapped his knife against his coffee bowl.

"I have a couple of announcements," he said. "We finally got the go-ahead to put in running water. So this very morning we start digging the trenches for the mains."

There was a mix of cheers and groans from around the table.

Kevin grinned. "Second, it's time to choose partners for the TVI pétanque tournament. It starts tomorrow afternoon. We want everyone taking part, from beginners to experts."

"What's that?" Frank whispered to Libby.

"It's a local game rather like lawn bowls," she whispered back. "You'll see."

Frank had no idea what lawn bowls were, either. Did they have something to do with coffee bowls?

"All right, that's it," Kevin concluded. "I'll see you in the square in half an hour."

Frank and Joe joined the others in clearing the table. Afterward they went outside and watched Jean-Claude and three others play pétanque. This involved tossing or rolling heavy steel balls as big as baseballs. The aim was to end up as close as possible to a little target ball. You also tried to hit your opponent's ball to knock it *away* from the target.

"I bet I can do that," Joe announced. "It's a lot like bowling, but without the pins or the hard floor."

"Will you team with me?" Marie-Laure asked him. "I am pretty good, and I think you will learn fast."

"Uh, sure," Joe said. Frank saw from his face that he was wondering what he was getting into.

The game finished and the teens went to work.

Kevin helped them lay out the course of the new water main with pegs and string. It ran from the top end of the village, under the shadow of the castle wall, to the lower end, near Sophie's office.

Frank, Joe, and a half dozen others started prying up cobblestones and carefully piling them to one side. As soon as the stones were cleared, another crew started digging a narrow trench.

The job went surprisingly quickly. A guy named Antonio taught the others a bouncy song from his region outside Rome. It fit perfectly with the rhythm

39

of the pickaxes and shovels. By ten o'clock the trench was already half the length of the first block of houses.

Frank was trying to get his pry bar under a very stubborn cobblestone when he was startled by a loud scream. He whirled around. Libby was standing with her head back and her arm extended upward. Frank looked where she was pointing.

Fifty feet above them, a block of stone as big as a large suitcase teetered on the top edge of the castle wall. For a long moment it seemed to balance there. Then it toppled forward. Trailing a tail of dust, it tumbled through the air toward the ground.

5 United Emanations

"Back!" Joe shouted. "Everybody back!"

"Quick!" Frank added.

Now others were shouting, too, in half a dozen languages. Libby was a few feet from Joe. The English girl seemed frozen in place by the sight of the plummeting stone. Joe grabbed her around the waist and pulled her toward the shelter of the nearest house.

The block of stone crashed down on a pile of rubble at the base of the castle wall. The impact sent a cloud of smaller stones and pebbles flying in all directions like buckshot. One grazed Joe's bare arm. When he looked down, he saw a line of red forming against his tan.

Libby was holding her palm against her cheek. "Are you hurt?" Joe asked her.

Her lips moved, but he didn't hear any words. He took her hand and gently moved it away from her face. There were no cuts, only a pinkness where she had been pressing her hand against it.

"I . . . I . . ." Libby stammered. "Up there. I saw him. Or . . . or something. It looked like a puff of smoke, but I *knew*. It was the spirit of the Sieur! He doesn't want us here. He is saying, 'Leave!' Or he'll drive us away."

A crowd gathered to listen to Libby. On their faces Joe saw a mixture of unease and doubt. Was the chateau really haunted?

"I, too, looked up when the stone fell," Manu said. "I saw no ghost. I think you imagine this."

Luis took Libby's side. "If she says she saw something, she did."

"This is just what I warned you about," Gert added. "The spirit of this place is angry with us."

"Nonsense," Marie-Laure said loudly. "There is no ghost here. This is my family's home since the days of Charlemagne. Would we stay in a place that is haunted?"

"You *didn't* stay," Gert pointed out. "Your family moved away from Fréhel after the Sieur was killed. You let the chateau fall into ruins. Your ancestors and the townspeople left because they were afraid of something they could not explain."

Before Marie-Laure could reply, her brother pushed forward. He stopped with his face just inches from Gert's. "You will stop this idiotic talk at once," he said through clenched teeth.

Gert's face reddened. "You will not tell me what to do," he retorted. "Your family does not rule here any longer. You are too arrogant."

"You dare to speak of arrogance?" Jean-Claude said. "*You?*" He gave an exaggerated laugh.

Joe put one hand on Gert's shoulder and the other on Jean-Claude's. "Okay, take it easy," he said. Gert tried to shrug him off. Joe tightened his grip.

"Joe's right," Frank said. "Arguing won't get us anywhere. Personally, I'd like to take a close look at the wall up there. A stone that size doesn't fall all by itself."

"Just my point," Gert said. He took a step back from Jean-Claude. Joe let go of his shoulder. "The Sieur's ghost must have pushed it."

"If he did," Joe said, "he's been working out at the Spookytown Gym. That looked like one heavy stone!"

Kevin came running up the street. "What happened?" he demanded. "Is anybody hurt?"

Welly explained, and a couple of times Gert seemed ready to chime in with his ghost theory. Joe thought that the scowl on Jean-Claude's face may have stopped him.

When Welly finished, Frank asked, "Can Joe and I

go up and look at the castle wall? I'd like to see if we can get an idea of how the stone fell."

Kevin gave him a shrewd look. "I've got no problem with that," he said. "But the chateau is private property. It's nothing to do with TVI."

"I'll take you," Jean-Claude offered.

"Be very careful," Gert said. "The ghost of the Sieur may decide to push you off the castle wall."

Jean-Claude turned away and muttered something in French. Joe guessed it meant, "I wish someone would push *you*."

The path to the chateau was steep and rocky. It ended at the edge of a dry ditch about eight feet deep and ten feet wide. A rickety wooden footbridge crossed the ditch to the chateau's main gate.

"This is the moat," Jean-Claude told them.

"I thought moats were filled with water," Joe said.

Jean-Claude laughed. "In Provence? You would have to be very rich indeed for that! No, the moat is simply to slow down anyone who attacks the chateau. If you withdraw the bridge, they must climb down one side and up the other. While they do, you can shoot arrows or drop things on them from above."

"Things like a big stone," Frank said.

Jean-Claude didn't reply. He led the way across the bridge and through the unbarred gate. Joe noticed a crooked sign tacked to a post near the bridge. The faded letters read:

44

Propriété Privée
Défense d'Entrer

The Hardys didn't need much French to translate that: "Private Property—Don't Enter." The sign didn't look likely to stop many trespassers.

Once past the gate, they had to walk through an arched tunnel.

"We are going under the guardroom now," Jean-Claude explained. "Once there were holes in the ceiling for shooting more arrows at invaders. They are blocked off since a long time. Watch where you step," he added.

Good advice but a little late. Joe had just bumped his foot on a rock.

The tunnel led to a big courtyard. High walls encircled it. Some of them had tall arched windows. Others were bleak, bare stone.

Frank looked around. "I'm confused," he admitted. "Aren't castles supposed to have pointy towers with walls around them? I see the wall, but where's the castle?"

"It is part of the wall," Jean-Claude said. "True, many old chateaux had a strong central building. It was called the donjon or keep. If the enemy got through the outer wall, the defenders could retreat to the keep and go on fighting."

"I remember that from a TV special about the Middle Ages," Joe contributed. "One castle had three different sets of walls *and* a keep."

"A royal castle, I think," Jean-Claude said. "Who but a king could afford enough men-at-arms to guard so many walls? Here at Fréhel, the cliffs were the first defense. Because of them, there was no real need to build a separate keep. My ancestors saved much effort by making the outer wall one of the sides of the living quarters. The great hall even has big windows that look out onto the village. You will see later."

"This place is fascinating," Frank said. "I'd love to take a closer look around. But right now, how do we get to where that stone fell from?"

"We have to go here," Jean-Claude replied. He led them around a corner and pointed.

Frank gulped. A series of squared-off stones stuck out from the wall. Each was higher and farther to the left than the one before it, to form a set of stairs. Some stones stuck out a couple of feet. Others were barely a foot wide. Here and there, gaps showed where a step had broken off altogether. Of course there was nothing like a handrail.

"You see why we cannot allow visitors," Jean-Claude said gravely. "If we ever decide to open the chateau to the public, we will first have to put in an ugly modern stairway."

"I'd hate to go up those steps in the dark," Joe said. "That'd be a good recipe for a broken neck."

Frank took the lead. The stones felt very solid. As long as he didn't look down, he was okay. Still, he gave a sigh of relief when he stepped onto the top of the wall.

The wall was wide enough for two people to walk side by side. The outer edge was about three feet higher than the walkway. Frank imagined bowmen leaning out to shoot arrows, then ducking back for protection from the besiegers' reply. He looked over the edge. The place the stone had landed was twenty feet over to the right.

"That way," Frank said. Joe was already ahead of him.

"Look at this!" Joe exclaimed. He pointed at the top of the wall. "These scratches are lighter than the rest of the stone. I think they're fresh."

"You're right," Frank said. "And this patch near the outer edge looks damp." He touched his fingertip to it. Definitely wet, and cool, too.

Joe bent down to pick up a short, thick piece of wood. The ends looked scraped, as if they had rubbed against something hard. "This could have been used as a prop," Joe said. "The same as that booby trap yesterday."

"Yes, but there's no string tied to this one," Frank replied. "What made the stone fall when it did? How's this . . . our baddie guy props the stone so it's tilted toward the edge. Then he shoves a block of ice under it to hold it up and takes the prop out. The ice melts, the stone tips over the edge, and *boom!*"

"Sounds good to me," Joe said. "So the guy comes

up here after breakfast and rigs the trap. Then he has plenty of time to go back down and establish an alibi before it falls."

"You fellows are something," Jean-Claude said admiringly. "Anyone would say you were real detectives!"

"Er—thanks," Frank said. "But if we're right, you see what it means. The guy had no way of knowing exactly when the stone would fall."

"Or whether someone would be in the way of it," Joe added. He rubbed the fresh scratch on his arm. "It's only luck that nobody was killed."

After lunch another game of pétanque was started. Joe stopped to watch. Marie-Laure was seated on the other side of the square. She waved, then pointed to a place next to her on the bench. Joe went over and sat down.

"If we are to be partners tomorrow," Marie-Laure said, "you must look and learn." She gave him an impish grin.

"I don't think that'll do it," Joe said. "I'll need some practice, too."

"I'll play with you this evening," Marie-Laure promised. "You will pick it up quickly, I know."

Joe let his eye wander over the sunlit houses, the narrow, crooked lanes, and the looming presence of the chateau. "This is quite a place," he said. "You must be really fond of it."

"Oh, yes," Marie-Laure said. "It means very much to me. To all my family. If only we can keep it from the hands of Immo-Trust . . ."

"Who's that?" Joe asked, puzzled.

Marie-Laure twisted her hands in her lap. "A very powerful firm of developers," she replied. "Parisians. They want to make Fréhel into a place for only the rich. They would put guards down in the valley to turn away ordinary people. If Sophie can raise enough money for TVI, there is no problem. But if not, we may have no choice. We may be forced to sell the entire property to Immo-Trust."

Joe remembered Marie-Laure's words that evening. According to custom, everyone went up to the ledge to watch the sunset. Before they returned to the village, Sophie said, "There is something you should all know. An important newspaper in Avignon has just printed a long article about Fréhel."

"That's super!" Welly said. "What did it say about TVI?"

"Nothing very good, I'm afraid," Sophie told him. "It deals mostly with history. It retells the legend that the Sieur's ghost haunts the village. Much talk about mysterious events and so on. Then it suggests that our program is close to collapse. It claims those in it are being frightened away."

"What nonsense!" Marina scoffed. "Anyone can see we are all still here."

Sophie nodded. "True. But many more people will

see the article than will see *us*. And those who have thought of supporting TVI with their contributions may think again. Will they want to throw their money away on a failing program?"

"This is a disaster!" Narguib declared. "What can we do?"

"Stay calm," Sophie replied. "If people from the media come to visit, show them the positive work we are doing. Tell them about the spirit of friendship and cooperation among young people from such varied countries."

"They can see all that for themselves," Antonio said. "They simply need to look."

"People don't always see what is in front of them," Manu pointed out. "Especially if they are hoping for something else."

"A very good point," Sophie said. "And of course they will be. They will be hoping for something to astonish and amaze their audience. That is why it is so important for us to avoid saying anything to suggest—"

"Look!" Luis suddenly exclaimed. "Up there!"

Joe spun around and stared up at the chateau. What was Luis so excited about?

Then he saw it. One of the tall window openings of the great hall was starting to brighten with a ghastly green color. A vague glowing form that was not human floated slowly across the opening.

Those around Joe started muttering in their different languages. Libby gasped and thrust the knuckles of her right hand between her teeth.

The form floated past a second window. Moments later it appeared over the wall of the chateau. Its movements became jerky and threatening. Suddenly it began to rise quickly, then dwindled into the evening sky and vanished.

In the silence that followed, Libby cried, "It was him! I saw his face! He hates us! He wants us all dead!"

6 Spook Hunt

Libby started to tremble. Sophie went over and put an arm around her.

"I am furious!" Jean-Claude announced loudly. "Whoever is responsible for this is my enemy and the enemy of TVI!"

"Even if it's your great-great-great-grandfather?" Gert asked.

Jean-Claude clenched his fists and took a step toward him. Frank moved between them. "That's not helpful," he told the German boy. "Who got a good look at that thing? Anyone?"

The others hesitated. During the silence, Frank scanned the circle of faces. Just as he thought—no one was missing. Either the incident was the work of an outsider, or it involved some sort of delayed action device. Unless, of course, they had just had an authentic visit from the ghost of the Sieur de Fréhel.

"It was huge," Welly said. "At least ten feet tall."

"No, no," Sari said. "I am sure it was no more than two or three feet high."

Some of the others laughed. Welly and Sari had such different impressions. Frank was not surprised. He was used to hearing eyewitnesses disagree about even the simplest detail.

"At least everyone saw it was green?" Manu asked.

"I'd say greenish white," Marina replied. "More white than green. Hardly green at all, in fact."

"What did you think of the sword of fire it was holding?" Antonio asked.

"What rubbish!" Welly said. "It wasn't holding anything!"

"Did *you* see a sword of fire?" Joe asked Antonio.

"Well . . . no," Antonio admitted. "I wondered how suggestible you are, that's all. In truth, I saw only something that glowed and moved. It looked like nothing in particular. But definitely green."

"This isn't getting us anywhere," Kevin said. "If any of you know something about this stunt, I hope you'll think long and hard. You could do serious damage to everything we're working for."

"I suggest we all go back and have a tisane," Sophie said. She noticed Frank's questioning look and added, "That's an herb tea. Whatever that thing was, it gave some of us a shock."

The group started down the path to the village. Frank and Joe fell in next to Marie-Laure and Jean-Claude.

"We'd like to look around the chateau," Frank announced.

"That does not astonish me," Jean-Claude said. "But now? Impossible. You must wait until morning."

"If there's anything that would show what really happened tonight, it may be gone by morning," Joe pointed out.

"I know that," Jean-Claude replied. "All the same, you must wait."

"The chateau is not so safe even when you have light to see well," Marie-Laure added. "I know it well since I was a baby. Even so, I would not go there by night. Say you do not fall through a hole in the floor. There are still the *vipères* that hide among the stones."

"But—" Joe began to say.

Marie-Laure gave him a roguish look. "Besides, tonight you must practice at pétanque. You promised!"

The *peep-peep-peep* of Frank's wrist alarm bored into his dream. He opened his eyes and brought the dial close to them. Five-thirty. He rolled over and looked toward the nearest window. It glowed with the pinkish gray of first light.

Frank climbed down from his bunk and touched Joe on the shoulder. Joe awoke instantly. They quickly pulled on shorts and T-shirts. Carrying their shoes, they crept down the stairs to the street. After a moment to slip on their shoes, they started up the hill toward the chateau.

As they crossed the footbridge to the entrance tunnel, Joe murmured, "How do we find the great hall? We haven't been there yet."

"We look for the biggest room," Frank replied, with a straight face. "No, seriously—it's behind those tall arched windows. How hard will that be to find?"

Not hard, as it turned out. The first doorway they entered led them to a huge roofless space with rows of windows on two sides. Oddly, the bottom edges of the windows were twelve feet up from the stone floor.

"Why are they so high?" Joe wondered. "Was this a chapel?"

"Look at the fireplace, down at the far end," Frank replied. It, too, was up from the ground. "There must have been another floor, about ten feet over our heads. It probably went the same time as the roof."

"So we're standing in the cellar," Joe said. "Weird."

Frank lowered his gaze from the walls and windows. "Hmm. This place has been abandoned for years, right?" he asked.

"Right," Joe said.

"Then tell me this," Frank continued. "How come the floor is so clean?"

Joe scanned the floor. Then he said, "Simple question, simple answer. Somebody swept it. Look. Over here you can still see the marks of a broom."

"And a pile of dust," Frank added. "So whoever swept wasn't worried about dirt. They were getting rid of traces they'd left. Footprints, whatever."

"Not all of them," Joe said, with excitement in his tone. "Look at this."

Frank joined him near the outer wall. At the edge of one of the flagstones was an odd spiral mark about six inches across. It looked scorched. In the center of the mark, a blackened thumbtack was stuck into a crack in the stone. A thin layer of gray ash covered the area.

Frank touched his fingertip to the ash, then smelled it. "Why am I thinking of backyard barbecues?" he wondered aloud.

"Because that looks like ashes from a charcoal grill," Joe responded. "Duh!"

"Uh-uh. That's not it," Frank said. "Here. Smell."

Joe sniffed the ashes. His face changed. "Hold on," he said. "It's that mosquito stuff. Like in candles. What's it called?"

"Citronella," Frank said. "You got it. And *that* has to be the mark left by one of those coils you burn to keep mosquitos away. Chet used them at his beach party a few weeks ago. Remember?"

"You're saying somebody had a picnic here?" Joe asked. He glanced around at the high stone walls. "Too much like a prison, if you ask me."

Frank pretended not to hear. "The thing with those coils is, they burn a long time," he said. "Half an hour or more. Yesterday morning our guy used ice to time his stunt. And this time I think he used fire."

Joe looked at the mark, then scanned the room. "Let me see if we're on the same page here," he said. "Whatever that was we saw last night, it was fastened to the mosquito coil. The coil was lit. It slowly burned. When the fire got to the right spot, it released the thingie."

"And by that time, whoever did it had already joined the crowd out on the ledge," Frank concluded.

"I wonder if it's Libby," Joe said. "She was doing her best to give us all the heebie-jeebies."

"She looked really scared to me," Frank replied. "But that gives me an idea . . . what if the real perp is getting at her? You know, playing on her fears so she'll help spook the rest of us."

"I hope not," Joe said. "That would be really nasty."

"Dropping big rocks near people isn't exactly tossing rose petals," Frank retorted. "We'd better get back. We don't want to miss breakfast."

* * *

Most of the others were already at the table when Joe and Frank arrived. Joe took a seat between Marina and Antonio. Frank was near the end on the same side, next to Welly.

"We have an excursion this morning," Marina said as Joe poured his coffee and milk. "Today is market day in Vaisac. Do you have a camera? It is very colorful."

"I forgot to bring one," Joe confessed. He reached for a croissant. It was still warm from the oven. "Where's Vaisac? Near here?"

"Not far," Marina said. "At night you can see the lights of the town from the chateau."

"You mean you go into the chateau at night?" Joe asked. "Isn't that dangerous?"

"Oh, not inside," Marina replied. "I meant from next to the chateau. By the way, I talked to my cousin in the US yesterday. I told her I'd just met two guys from Bayport. I wondered if she knew you."

"And?" Joe asked.

"She doesn't," Marina said. With an odd look, she added, "But she thought she'd heard of you."

Joe could imagine. Some of his and Frank's successful cases had caused a lot of stir. Should he ask Marina to keep to herself whatever her cousin had told her? Or would that just make a bigger deal of it? Before he could decide, Luis, on Marina's other side, started a conversation with her.

After breakfast everyone gathered at the parking

lot. The first ones there smugly installed themselves in Kevin's air-conditioned van. Joe and Frank followed the others into the rear of the old Citroën. They all sat on the floor and leaned back against the metal side walls.

The drive down the hill reminded Joe of an amusement park ride—an old, rickety ride, long overdue for repairs. Every stone they drove over—and there were lots of them—bounced him into the air. The truck lurched alarmingly to one side, then the other. The engine sounded like the Hardys' old lawn mower.

Joe looked around for something to grab on to. The others were laughing as they bounced and lurched. This must be normal, then. He relaxed. After a moment he managed to think of the trip as fun.

Twenty minutes later the Citroën lurched to a halt. The *putt-putt* of the engine stopped. Narguib, at the very rear, pushed the double doors open. They all climbed out.

The truck was parked in a wide square with tall trees around the edges. Across the nearest street, the buildings of the old town rose in levels up the side of a hill. Massive old stone walls and a modern-looking chapel crowned the hill.

The Fréhel twins came over. "This is a very historic place," Jean-Claude told Joe and Frank. "The counts of Vaisac once ruled all the lands around here. The daughter of one married the king of France."

"So where's this supermarket we're going to?" Joe asked. He looked around for a store sign. "What makes it so special?"

Marie-Laure held back a laugh. "Not a supermarket," she said. "A market. Every Wednesday farmers come to town. They bring their best produce to sell from stands in the streets. People from all around come to shop and to see their friends. For many it is the high point of the week."

Joe raised his head and sniffed the air. "Speaking of high points, I could swear I smell pizza," he announced.

Jean-Claude indicated a van parked nearby. The rear was open, with a counter across it. A metal chimney protruded through the roof. "Baked to order in a wood-fired brick oven," he said proudly. "Before we leave, you must try it."

"Why wait?" Joe replied. Frank grabbed his arm and pulled him away.

The narrow, winding streets of the old town had been closed to cars. Two thick streams of shoppers flowed between the lined-up stalls. When one stout man stopped to buy purple onions, he brought everyone to a halt.

Joe took the moment to look around. The nearest stall was heaped with colorful fruit—plums, peaches, and dark red cherries. At the next one, cages of live chickens and rabbits were stacked three high. Beyond that was a stand draped with cowboy-style shirts in blinding colors and patterns.

Traffic started moving again. Around the next bend, Frank stopped at a stand that displayed a dozen different varieties of honey. The woman behind the counter dipped bits of bread in a pot labeled *Miel de Lavande*. She offered them to Frank and Joe. It tasted like a cross between honey and fresh flowers.

"What do you think?" Frank asked. "Get some for Mom and Dad?"

Joe imagined how good the honey would taste on pancakes and English muffins. "Sure," he said with a grin. "But they'll have to work fast if they want any of it!"

Frank bought a jar of the honey. The woman insisted on wrapping it in colorful paper. While they waited, Joe scanned the crowd. All the others from TVI had drifted away. Was that Marie-Laure up ahead, turning into a side street?

"I'll be right back," Joe told Frank. He started walking. He tried to move faster than the crowd, but it was no good. Even his skills as a broken field runner were of little help. By the time he got to the side street, the girl he had spotted was out of sight.

Joe shrugged and turned back to rejoin Frank. As he walked past a shadowy archway, he was sure he heard someone say something about TVI. He stopped and looked around. A few feet away, a young woman he didn't recognize was standing with her back to him. She seemed to be talking, in accented English, to someone inside the arched passage.

Joe started to walk on, but at that moment he heard the woman say, "You *must* frighten them off. TVI must fail—and quickly. Whatever it takes, do it. Do you understand? If someone is hurt, too bad!"

7 Head-on Collision

The ominous words echoed in Joe's head. "If some-one is hurt, too bad!" This was his chance to find out who had rigged those booby traps. He tried to get a glimpse of whomever the woman was talking to. No luck. His eyes were too adapted to the bright sun-light of the street. All he could see inside the dark passage was the vague form of a person. He or she was starting to move away, down the passage.

Desperately, Joe darted forward. At that moment, a little knot of shoppers crossed in front of him. He crashed into a woman with a straw basket of vegeta-bles on her arm. A paper bag of carrots flew out and burst on the cobblestones.

"Sorry!" Joe exclaimed. He bent down to collect the carrots. "Excuse me!"

The woman glared at him. She grabbed the carrots out of his hand and thrust them in her basket. As she stalked away, she said something loudly to a man near her. The only word Joe caught was "touriste." He could guess from her tone that the rest was not friendly.

The young woman he had overheard was still standing at the mouth of the passage. She had obviously noticed Joe's collision with the shopper. She seemed to think it was funny.

Joe pretended to look past her while he quickly memorized her appearance. She was wearing a dark blue skirt, a white silk blouse, and a blue print scarf knotted in her blond hair. Designer sunglasses hid her eyes. Her face was carefully made up, and the dark red polish on her nails had been applied by a skilled hand.

The woman started up the street, past Joe. Still not looking at her, he took a few steps in the opposite direction. Then he turned. She was well ahead, with a big clump of people between them. Joe went after her. He walked slowly. He did not dare get so close that she might notice him. She was his only lead at this point.

Twice Joe was sure he had lost her in the crowded, narrow streets. Each time his height let him peer over the heads of the crowd and spot the blond hair and blue scarf. At last she turned under a carved archway that led out onto the main square. She walked over to a glossy late-model sports car, climbed in, and drove off.

Joe had a felt-tip pen in his pocket. He grabbed it and wrote the number of the car's license plate on his bare forearm. He wasn't likely to lose *that!*

The next job was to find Frank and fill him in. Joe retraced his steps. The market was nearly over. The farmers and other stallholders were starting to pack whatever they hadn't sold. The stream of shoppers had turned to flow downhill. The terraces of the cafés were jammed with people enjoying little cups of espresso or brightly colored cold drinks.

At one of the cafés, Joe noticed Manu, Marina, and Libby. They waved and pointed to an empty chair. Joe smiled and shook his head. "Have you seen my brother?" he called.

Marina thought a moment. Then she nodded and gestured up the street. Joe waved his thanks and started edging his way through the oncoming crowd. It was slow going. He wondered if he should return to the van and wait for Frank there. Then he felt a tap on his shoulder.

"What happened to you?" Frank's familiar voice asked. "Get lost?"

Joe turned. "No. But I think I almost got a look at the booby trapper." He explained and showed Frank the license plate number.

"I wonder how we find out who that belongs to," Frank said. "Maybe Dad knows somebody who could help. Do you have his new number with you?"

Most American cell phones used a different system than in Europe. Before leaving Bayport, Fenton Hardy had got a multistandard cell phone that would work abroad.

Joe dug through his wallet and found the number. "I saw some phone booths in the post office," he said. "A block or so back that way."

The telephone in the wood-lined booth felt as solid as a tank. It had one old-fashioned feature Joe appreciated—a second earphone. Frank made the call, but Joe could listen to both sides of the conversation.

Their father answered right away. Frank explained what they wanted.

"Oof!" Fenton said. "French bureaucrats are famous for being surly and uncooperative. They don't even help each other if they can avoid it. But I'll see what I can do. There's a fellow in the Sûreté who owes me a favor. How do I get back to you?"

"We're in town now, but we're heading back to TVI pretty soon," Frank replied. "Could you call the office and leave a message for us to call you? Tell them you're our dad. They'll be sure to pass it on."

"Will do," Fenton said. "And I expect to hear all about whatever you've got yourselves into."

"For sure!" Frank told him. "How's your conference going?"

"It's fascinating," Fenton said. "Every time the UN eliminates one way of getting illegal diamonds into Europe, the smugglers come up with two or three new ones. The only real cure will be to make dealers check the origin of every single stone they buy. If the smugglers can't sell their goods, they'll have to close up shop."

"Any chance that'll happen?" Frank wondered.

"It's happening already," Fenton replied. "If I were a diamond smuggler, I'd start looking for a new line of work."

Joe and Frank returned to the square. Most of the others were already waiting near the two vans. Jean-Claude noticed Frank's packages. "Oho!" he chuckled. "I am glad to see you are supporting the economy of Provence with American dollars."

"What did you buy?" Marie-Laure asked.

"A wooden herb grinder and two jars of lavender honey," Frank replied. "They'll make great gifts."

"I love lavender honey," Marie-Laure enthused. "I love anything with the scent of lavender. I use lavender cologne all the time."

Joe nodded to himself. When he had tasted the honey, he thought it reminded him of something. Now he knew what—Marie-Laure's perfume.

"Look what I found," Narguib said. He held up a black T-shirt with the familiar emblem of the Chicago Bulls. "Isn't that something? I'm a very big fan."

Joe noticed the words on the T-shirt. They read, *Chicago Bills*. Should he tell Narguib his new shirt was a fake? Not without thinking it over, that was for sure.

The rest of the group straggled up. Joe clambered into the back of the Citroën and sat next to Marie-Laure. He noticed her scent. It was very nice, not too heavy, like a stroll through a field. He should ask where she got it and take some home for presents.

Everybody settled down for the trip back to Fréhel. "So what did you guys do at the market?" Joe asked. He hoped the answers would give a clue to the name of the person in the passageway.

"We wandered and looked," Marina replied. "Then we sat and watched the people go by."

"It's so interesting," Libby added. "I could spend whole days at a French café!"

"As for me," Siri said, "I became very lost. By luck, I found Welly and Luis. They showed me the way back."

Frank picked up on Joe's cue. "How did you guys manage to stay together?" he asked. "That crowd was really thick."

"I kept my eye on Welly," Luis replied. "Not so many people here are very tall and black."

Joe thought back. Had the person in the passage been much taller than average? He didn't think so. They could probably cross Welly off their list of suspects. That pleased him. He liked the big South African. And if Welly and Luis were together the whole time, that eliminated Luis as well.

Before Joe or Frank could pose any more questions, Narguib and Luis started a conversation about the pétanque tournament that was to start after lunch.

"Jean-Claude will win easily," Luis proclaimed. "He is the only one who has played boules before this summer."

"He is not!" Marie-Laure said indignantly.

"Oh—sorry," Luis said. "I meant he and you, of course. But he is partnered with Libby. At least she has played since she came to TVI. No offense, Joe, but you do not become good at boules in one day."

"What's boules?" Joe asked.

"Another name for pétanque," Marie-Laure explained. "*Pétanque* is the word in Provençal. That's the language people used to speak in this region."

"Some people still speak it," Jean-Claude added. "When I go to the university, I intend to study Provençal. The old poetry is very beautiful."

At lunch Sophie made an announcement. "On Friday evening the children of the *colonie de vacances* near Vaissade will visit us. They will tour Fréhel and see what we do here."

Siri raised her hand. "Excuse me, but what is this *colonie?*"

Marie-Laure answered. "It is a place for children

from the city to be in the countryside during the school vacation."

"Summer camp," Frank muttered under his breath. Joe flashed him a grin.

"In the evening," Sophie continued, "we will make an entertainment for them. Kevin will organize it."

Kevin stood up. "This is your big break, people," he said. "We need volunteers to be part of the show. Who plays an instrument?"

Libby slowly raised her hand. "I play guitar," she said. "I could sing some English folk songs."

"Great. Who else?" Kevin's gaze made the rounds of the table. "Siri? What about you?"

"Oh, I do not sing at all," Siri said quickly. "I could tell a story from my country, if that would be interesting."

"You're on," Kevin said, jotting on a notepad. "But we need more."

"I am a clown," Luis offered.

"We know that already," Welly cracked.

"No, I mean it," Luis told him. "At home I put on a costume and makeup. I go to the children's hospital. I juggle and fall over and do funny walks. Then I make things from balloons and give them to the children."

"Wonderful," Sophie said. "Perfect!"

Kevin nodded and made another note. "So far we've got a folksinger, a storyteller, and a clown. This is shaping up nicely. Does anybody dance?"

"I know some Provençal folk dances," Marie-Laure said. "I could teach them to the children. And my brother is a wonderful whistler."

Jean-Claude gave her a dirty look, then said, "Okay, sure."

"And how about a demonstration of martial arts?" Joe suggested. "Frank and I could do that."

Frank cleared his throat loudly. Joe refused to look at him.

"Okay," Kevin said. "The rest of you have a couple of days to get over your shyness. Just let me know. Believe me, the kids from Vaissade will love whatever you do."

After lunch everyone went out to the square. Kevin tacked up a schedule for the first round of the pétanque tournament. The others crowded around to study it. Joe saw that he and Marie-Laure were matched with Manu and Marina.

"Do they play this game in Belgium or Greece?" he whispered to Marie-Laure. "If not, we've got a shot."

"We are going to win," Marie-Laure replied. Her gaze dared him to disagree. "Simply do whatever I tell you."

Before the game could start, Sophie came back up the hill. She beckoned to Joe and Frank. They went over to her.

"There is a message from your father on the *répondeur,*" she announced. "He would like you to call him in Paris."

71

"May we use the office phone?" Frank asked. "We'll be glad to pay the charges."

"Of course," Sophie said. "The door is open."

Fenton answered on the second ring. Frank held the receiver so that Joe could hear, too.

"I got the information you wanted," Fenton announced. "I hope it's what you need. I had to move a couple of mountains to get it."

"Great, Dad," Frank said. He got his pen and notepad ready. "We really appreciate it."

"Now then," Fenton continued. "The license plate number you gave me doesn't belong to a person. It's registered to a company here in Paris."

Joe's heart sank. What if it was a rental car? They might never manage to trace the driver.

"I've never heard of the outfit," Fenton said. "But my friend in the Sûreté says it's got a lot of clout down where you are. Funny name—it's called Immo-Trust."

8 A Breach of Trust

Frank replaced the phone receiver. Slowly he turned to face Joe. "Immo-Trust," he said. "We've heard that name before."

"Right," Joe said. "That's the developer Jean-Claude told us about. The bunch that wants to buy the chateau and village and turn them into a ritzy resort complex."

Frank felt a mixture of sadness and anger. He pushed it out of his mind. He needed to stay clear-headed. "One of the kids here has to be working for them," he said, "trying to destroy the program, so that the Fréhels have to sell."

"Looks that way," Joe agreed. "Those sentences I overheard—what else could they mean? But who?"

"Not the twins," Frank said. "No motive. And we

eliminated Welly and Luis because they were together the whole time at the market."

"Unless they're *both* working for Immo-Trust," Joe pointed out. "But then why would one cover for the other? They've got no way of knowing I overheard that conversation."

"I guess we cross off Libby, Marina, and Manu, too," Frank said. "Same argument—they were together."

"I wonder," Joe said slowly. "Let's say Libby and Marina are doing the market together. Libby stops at one of the stalls, Marina walks on ahead. A few minutes later Libby catches up or Marina comes back."

"Okay," Frank said. He thought he saw where Joe was going with this. "And?"

"Unless they're, like, being grilled on a witness stand, they're both going to say they were together the whole time," Joe said. "And they'll think they were. But the fact is, either one could have slipped away long enough for a quick meeting with someone."

"Such as the woman from Immo-Trust," Frank said. "You know what, Joe? I really wish you hadn't thought of that. We were narrowing it down to a few suspects. Now it's wide open again. Hey, *I* could have met with her, after I bought the honey!"

"We could question people again," Joe suggested. "And get really picky about their answers."

"That's true," Frank replied. He thought for a

moment. "The thing is, for now nobody knows we're on the case. The culprit has no idea we're after him. That may give us a big advantage. But if we start asking a lot of questions . . ."

"He'll get suspicious and start covering his tracks better," Joe said, finishing Frank's sentence. "So what do we do? Nothing? Sit back and let this turkey destroy TVI?"

"For now, we watch and listen," Frank said. "And we talk with people. How about we each take half of them to concentrate on? Then we can compare notes later."

"Good idea," Joe said. "I'll take Marie-Laure."

Frank interrupted. "I thought you might," he said with a grin.

"We're teammates, that's all," Joe said. "Which reminds me—"

"Ah, you are here!" Gert said from the doorway. "I was sent to find you. It is time for your game."

Frank and Joe exchanged a glance. Then they walked up the hill with Gert. The others were all in the square for the tournament.

The match between Siri and Luis versus Welly and Valentina, the girl from Madrid, was just starting. Valentina drew a line in the dirt, then threw the little wooden ball. It landed thirty feet away, near a clump of bushes.

Siri stepped up to the line. Scrunching up her face in concentration, she rolled the steel ball. It slowed to a stop less than halfway to the target. *"Aie!"* Siri exclaimed.

"Don't worry," Luis assured her. "We'll get better."

It was Welly's turn. Instead of rolling the ball, he lobbed it in a shallow arc. It slammed down only a foot or so from the target ball. Some onlookers started to cheer. But once on the ground, the heavy ball started to roll. By the time it came to rest, it was as far on the other side of the goal as Siri's was on this side.

"This looks tricky," Joe said in an undertone to Frank.

"Remember, it's not our game," Frank replied. "Nobody expects us to be good at it. Just don't hit anybody with one of those balls."

"Or drop one on my foot," Joe added.

Marie-Laure came over, carrying a set of steel balls in a red plastic holder. "Are you ready?" she asked. "Manu and Marina are waiting." She pointed to the opposite side of the square.

"Sure," Joe said jauntily. "Let's do it."

Marina tossed the target ball. It landed at the top of a little rise and rolled down the far slope. When it stopped, it was almost hidden from them.

Joe went first. Should he roll the ball or throw it? He glanced at Marie-Laure.

"Aim to land halfway there," she murmured. "Hold the ball with your hand on top. It will not roll as fast."

Joe stepped up to the line. He swung his arm back and forth a couple of times. The ball felt like nothing he was used to. It was the size of a baseball, but with almost the heft of a bowling ball. He fixed his eye on a spot halfway to the target and let fly.

The instant the ball left his hand, he knew he had put too much force into the throw. *"Aargh!"* he growled.

The ball landed and rolled off to the left. Gert and Antonio had to jump out of the way. By the time it stopped, it was at least a couple of dozen feet past the target.

Manu's turn. He narrowed his eyes, clenched his jaw, and gave the ball a gentle toss. It landed just a few feet from the target and rolled until it was almost touching the little wooden ball. Manu beamed and exchanged a high five with Marina.

Marie-Laure scowled. This was her game. She clearly did not intend to lose. She held the ball in her palm and tossed it up and down. Then, with no preparation that Joe could see, she threw it. It made a high arc, almost brushing a low tree branch. Joe was sure it would overshoot badly.

Sprang! The ball came down exactly in the little space between Manu's ball and the target. It struck both of them. Manu's ball shot away in one direction, the target in the other.

Joe felt his jaw drop. So *that* was how the game was played!

By the time the game ended, Joe was getting a feel for the ball. More often than not, it ended up somewhere near where he meant it to go. Even so, he knew that it was Marie-Laure alone who carried their side. Time after time, she placed her ball next to the target or struck one of his so that it rolled next to the target. Both Manu and Marina played pretty well—better than Joe—but they didn't stand a chance against the French girl.

The morning excursion to Vaisac and the pétanque match during siesta had been fun, but now it was time to get serious. The teens collected their tools and returned to digging the water main trench. After the uncertainties of pétanque, Joe found the work almost comforting. When you stuck your shovel in the dirt, it usually went where you aimed it.

Marina was working next to Joe. "So far this is a good day," she remarked. "Nothing has happened."

"What do you mean?" Joe asked cautiously.

"Haven't you noticed?" Marina continued. "Every day there is something. Falling stones, strange floating lights . . . do you believe in ghosts?"

"Not really," Joe replied. "Do you?"

Marina considered for a moment. "I believe there is much in the world we do not understand. But spirits who float around going, *Woo, woo*? I don't think so." She lowered her voice. "Is that why you and your brother came here? To find out what is going on?"

Joe gave her a sharp glance and didn't speak.

"It's all right," Marina murmured. "I can keep a secret. I won't ask anything more."

Later, as everyone gathered for dinner, Joe kept Frank back. He repeated his conversation with Marina.

"I was afraid of that," Frank said. "Her American cousin must have said something about our detective work."

"I think she'll keep it to herself," Joe offered. He flinched as a sudden strong gust of wind peppered them with sharp grains of sand. Instead of dying down, the wind grew stronger and steadier. "Hey, I can't believe I'm getting chilly. Let's go inside."

Frank went to the door of the community center and pushed. The force of the wind held it closed. Joe had to help. As they went in, the wind tore the door from their hands and slammed it shut.

Welly was watching. Over the clamor of the wind whistling past the building, he asked, "Is this your first mistral? That's what they call this wind."

"Does it blow like this a lot?" Frank asked.

Welly shook his head. "This is just the second time since I've been here. But once it gets going, it hangs on. They say it blows either one day, or three days, or five days. If it lasts for seven days, people start going crazy from the noise."

"I believe it," Joe said.

79

The talk at dinner was mostly about the wind. "This is just a little taste," Jean-Claude proclaimed. "In winter the mistral can blow so strong it rips tiles off the roofs. And the noise! People stop trying to talk. Instead they write notes to each other."

"The reason the houses are so close together," Marie-Laure added, "is for protection from the mistral."

"The racket it makes is quite spooky," Welly said. "You can almost hear voices in it."

Libby turned pale. "I hear them!" she exclaimed. "Listen! There's something out there! It's trying to get inside!"

Everyone started talking at once, trying to calm Libby. But a moment later, as if on signal, they all became quiet. The howls of the wind filled the silence. Joe cocked his head toward the nearest window. Then he looked at Frank and frowned.

Libby was right. Among all the noises of the wind, he could pick out cries and moans that sounded human. They were getting louder and clearer, too.

Kevin sprang up from his chair. "Okay, what's going on here?" he demanded. "This is not funny!"

Now all of them were on their feet, looking scared. The noise level rose another notch. Panic was just around the corner.

Joe raised his arms over his head. "Hold it!" he shouted. "Pipe down, everybody!"

Everyone turned to stare at him. A silence fell. Joe motioned to Frank. The two of them slowly circled the room in opposite directions, turning their heads from side to side.

Joe came to a stop in front of the china cabinet. He jerked the doors open. The moans grew louder. He groped around behind the stacked plates. Nothing on the top shelf. On the next one down, he felt something that didn't belong.

He pulled it out. It was a portable tape player. He pressed the Stop button. On command, the moans stopped.

Joe turned and held up the tape player. "Here's our ghost," he announced.

"Hey, that's mine!" Welly exclaimed. "What's it doing here?"

"Trying to scare us," Kevin replied. "All right, who's the joker?"

Nobody spoke. People turned and looked at one another.

"I must warn whoever is responsible," Sophie said. "These pranks could threaten all our work. Unless they stop, the person behind them will be told to leave at once."

The only sounds were the rattling of the windows and the howl of the mistral.

Joe woke up abruptly. He opened his eyes. The room was dark. The glowing dial of his watch told him it was a few minutes after one. What had awakened him? Some noise outside? Then he understood. Not a noise, but a silence. The mistral had stopped blowing.

With a shrug, Joe rolled over to go back to sleep. At that moment he heard furtive footsteps in the street. Who would be sneaking around the village at this hour? He sprang up and went to the window. He was just in time to spot two figures vanish up the path to the chateau.

Three minutes later Joe and Frank were hurrying up the path. Frank had a pocket flash, but they didn't need it in the moonlight. They crept across the footbridge and through the entrance tunnel. In the courtyard they paused to look around.

"There!" Frank whispered. He pointed to a faint gleam of light. It came from one of the windows of the great hall.

The Hardys slipped across the courtyard and into the building. The corridor was pitch-black, but a faint glimmer outlined the doorway to the great hall. Joe breathed through his mouth as they tiptoed to the door and peered around the jamb.

The hall was empty. On the floor in the middle of the room was a lit flashlight.

A trap! Joe started to turn. Suddenly he felt an arm encircle his neck. It tightened in a choke hold.

9 Night Birds

The attacker's arm closed around Joe's neck. Joe reached up and grasped the forearm with both hands, then dropped to one knee. As he shifted his weight, preparing to throw the attacker over his shoulder, he caught a whiff of a familiar scent. In that same instant, he heard an alarmed *"Aie!"* next to his ear.

"Marie-Laure?" he gasped. "Is that you?"

"Joe!" Marie-Laure replied. She relaxed her arm and wriggled out of his grip.

Joe straightened up and took a quick look to his left.

Frank had a hammerlock on Jean-Claude. He released it and took a cautious step backward. Jean-Claude groaned and slumped to his knees.

"Oh!" Marie-Laure cried. "You've hurt him!" She rushed over to her brother. After a quick whispered exchange, she helped him to his feet.

Marie-Laure turned to face Joe. Her eyes blazed. "How dare you!" she exclaimed. "What are you doing here? Why did you follow us? Answer me!"

Joe took a deep breath. "Does it matter that *you* tried to jump *us?*" he asked bitterly.

"We saw someone sneaking up here," Frank explained. "After everything that's happened, we figured they were up to no good. So we came after them."

"And all we knew was that somebody was following us," Jean-Claude said. He rubbed his neck. "So we decided to entrap them. Not a very bright idea, it seems."

Marie-Laure was still angry. "Why not?" she demanded. "They are trespassers. We should order them to leave at once!"

Jean-Claude gave her a quirky look. "And if they refuse? Will you try again to strangle Joe? I think not. And after what just happened, I promise Frank that he is safe from me!"

Jean-Claude walked into the great hall and switched off the flashlight. Frank, Joe, and Marie-Laure followed. They could still see one another. Moonlight flooded in through the open space where the roof had once been.

"Look, we're not your enemies," Frank said. "We

want to stop these dirty tricks and find out who's in back of them."

Marie-Laure gave him a skeptical look. "Why should we believe you?" she asked. "And why do you believe you can do this?"

Joe met Frank's eyes. He raised one eyebrow. Should they trust the French brother and sister? Frank hesitated, then nodded.

"Listen," Joe said. "The fact is, Frank and I have had a lot of experience solving mysteries. Back home, we're pretty well known as detectives."

"I *knew* there was something out of the ordinary about you," Marie-Laure said.

"Why did you not say this before?" Jean-Claude asked.

"It might have sounded too much like bragging," Frank explained. "And then we saw something was going on here. We didn't want to alert the bad guys and put them on their guard."

"So you are already, as they say, on the case," Jean-Claude said. "Good. We need whatever help we can get."

"Help with what?" Joe asked. "What are you doing here in the middle of the night, anyway?"

It was Jean-Claude's and Marie-Laure's turn to exchange a questioning glance. They quickly reached a decision.

"We have been searching for our ancestor's treasure," Jean-Claude confessed. "Please don't laugh."

"The treasure is real," Marie-Laure said earnestly. "And we are sure it is still here somewhere. Or we were. We have looked very hard and found nothing."

"Do you have any clues?" Joe asked. "A map or something?"

Jean-Claude shook his head. "Nothing. Only the story you have heard already. The Sieur had no time to pass a message to his family before he died at the hands of the bandits. Someone—a servant perhaps—may have known where it was hidden. If so, he told no one. Perhaps he took it secretly and kept it for himself. He may have thought that, with the Sieur dead, it belonged to whoever found it."

"I am sure it is still in the chateau," Marie-Laure said. She placed her hand at the base of her neck. "I feel it *here!*"

Jean-Claude started to speak, but she continued. "And I am not alone. The one who is stalking us, he, too, knows the treasure is here."

"What do you mean?" Frank asked. "Who's stalking you?"

"We do not know," Jean-Claude told him. "It may be we are imagining it. But we have both sensed that someone is watching us. And I do not think it is our guardian angel. It is someone who does not wish us well."

"The one I overheard at the market!" Joe exclaimed.

"What is this?" Marie-Laure demanded.

Joe explained. When he'd finished, Jean-Claude said, "Of course! If we find the treasure, we will be able to save Fréhel from the grasp of Immo-Trust. Their agent will do anything to stop us. Just as he will do anything to wreck the reputation of TVI. But who is he?"

"We don't know," Frank admitted. "Yet. We're working on it."

"Let us help," Marie-Laure pleaded. "What can we do?"

"For now, keep your eyes and ears open," Frank suggested. "And tell us anything that feels odd or out of place."

Joe added, "And next time you decide to sneak around in the middle of the night, warn us. We need our beauty sleep."

Jean-Claude yawned so widely that the hinges of his jaw gave a loud click. "We promise," he said. "I wonder . . . are we foolish to put so much hope on a mythical treasure? Our grandfather liked to quote the motto on the Fréhel crest: True wealth is found around the family hearth. I think that may be very wise."

The four left the chateau and started back to the village. Frank touched Joe's arm in a silent signal. They slowed down to let Jean-Claude and Marie-Laure get well ahead of them.

"What?" Joe asked quietly.

"Just a thought," Frank replied. "If TVI is a success, the Fréhel family has pledged to turn the village over to the organization. That leaves them owning a useless chateau that needs very expensive repairs. But if TVI fails, what then? The family sells the village and chateau to Immo-Trust for a lot of money. *And* they get to tell all their friends they were forced into it."

Joe stopped and put his hand on Frank's arm. "Are you saying the ones working with Immo-Trust to wreck TVI are Jean-Claude and Marie-Laure? That's ridiculous!"

"Probably," Frank responded. "I hope so. But we can't ignore the possibility. They do have a motive, one of the most powerful around. Wealth."

"Sometimes I wish there was no such thing as wealth," Joe grumbled. "It causes nothing but grief!"

Frank finished breakfast and sat back in his chair. He felt a little sleepy from the midnight excursion to the chateau. It had been worth it, though. He and Joe now had answers to a few of their questions. With hard work and a little luck, this day might bring even more answers.

Sophie stood up and tapped her bowl. "A load of pipe arrives this morning," she announced. "It will have to be unloaded, moved onto the lift, and stacked at the upper end. Very strenuous work. Any volunteers?"

Hands shot up around the table. Frank's and Joe's were among them.

Sophie gave a satisfied nod. "Very good! Ah— Welly, Libby, Luis, Manu, Joe, and Frank. Welly, will you organize the job?"

"Sure," Welly said. "We'll handle it."

"Next," Sophie continued. "The talent show tomorrow night, for the children from the colonie. First rehearsal at eleven-thirty, in the square. Those involved will leave work early."

Several people cheered. Sophie smiled, then added, "And after lunch, we have the next round in the grand competition at pétanque."

"Why not just give the prize to Fréhel and be done with it," Gert muttered under his breath.

Marie-Laure heard him. "There is more than one Fréhel here," she retorted. "We both play pétanque. And we both have been taught to be good sports, whether we win or lose. Too bad there are some who never learned that lesson!"

Gert's face reddened. He looked on the point of making an angry response. Luis, sitting next to him, put a hand on his shoulder. "Take it easy," he advised. "Nothing to get upset over."

Gert pressed his lips together and let out his breath loudly. He made a show of standing up and stomping out of the dining room. A moment later the outer door was slammed.

Frank glanced around the table. The other teens

looked embarrassed by Gert's display of temper. None of them seemed very sympathetic to the German boy. Was that why he was so constantly on edge? Because he knew he was not well liked? But it was mostly his attitude that kept him from being liked.

After breakfast Frank, Joe, and the four others on the pipe detail hiked down the hill to the parking area. The truck from the plumbing supply house had not yet arrived.

"How is this?" Welly said. "All of us take the pipe off the truck. Then we split up. Three down here, to put it on the lift. Three up above, to take it off the lift and stack it."

"Sounds good," Frank said. The others nodded.

Manu went over to a motorcycle parked near the foot of the path. "Would anyone like a ride while we wait?" he asked.

"Is that yours?" Joe asked. "Cool!"

"It is old but very fast," Manu replied. "I rebuilt the engine myself." A helmet dangled from the handlebar. He reached inside and produced a key ring.

"You don't leave the ignition key there all the time, do you?" Libby asked. "Aren't you afraid someone will steal the bike?"

Manu gave her a puzzled look. "I would not do it in a city like Brussels or Antwerp," he replied. "But here we are all friends. We do not steal each other's property. If someone needs to borrow my moto, I give them permission in advance."

"May I take a spin?" Frank asked.

Manu handed him the helmet. Frank put it on and mounted up. The kick starter was stiff. He had to stand on it twice. Then the engine caught. It rumbled with a note of barely held-in power. He gave the throttle a careful nudge and let in the clutch. The motorcycle jumped forward like a scalded cat.

It took Frank a moment to find his balance. He aimed the bike along the edge of the parking lot and gave it more gas. As he raced in a big circle, he felt the wind tug his lips into a devilish grin.

"Wa-hooo!" he shouted as he sped past the others. They smiled and waved. Frank started into his second lap. Then he noticed a truck struggling up the track from the valley. That must be the load of water pipe. He slowed his pace, rode back to the starting point, and parked the motorcycle.

"Thanks. That was great," Frank told Manu. He hung the helmet on the handlebar and tucked the key inside.

The truck driver parked near the bottom of the lift. Joe and Welly jumped onto the back and started passing the sections of pipe down. Each one was about six inches wide and five feet long.

The pipe was too heavy for one person to carry. Frank paired off with Libby. Joe and Welly handed them a section. While they carried it to the lift, Luis and Manu lined up to take the next section.

It was hard work, but it went fast. Soon half a dozen sections were loaded on the platform of the lift. The others were neatly stacked next to it.

"Luis? Joe?" Welly said. "We will go up the hill to unload. Libby, Manu, and Frank will stay here to load what is left."

Frank was disappointed not to be with Welly. He had hoped to use the casual setting to question him about his tape machine. Who knew he had one? Who had access to it? When had Welly used it last? And could you record on it? If not, where had the prankster taped those moans and cries?

Joe and the others started up the path. Libby flipped the switch to start the lift on its way up. It creaked and groaned under the heavy load. By the time it reached the top, the three guys were there, ready for it. Just minutes later they sent the empty platform down again.

Frank and his coworkers had just loaded the last of the pipe and were watching it make its way up the hill when they heard a noise.

"Listen!" Libby said. "That's the bell. But it's not lunchtime. Something must have happened!"

The three hurried up the path to the village. A crowd had gathered in front of the community center. Kevin was standing next to the door. He had a smile on his face and an old wooden box under his arm.

Frank spotted Joe and gave him a questioning look. Joe shrugged and shook his head.

"Is everybody here?" Kevin asked. He scanned the crowd. "I want you all to be the first to know. This morning a dream of mine came true. I just found this inside my cottage. Look!"

He pried up the lid of the wooden box. Inside were hundreds of small clear stones that gleamed in the sunlight.

"Diamonds!" Kevin proclaimed. "A fortune in diamonds!"

10 Buried Treasure

Everyone stared openmouthed at the box of diamonds Kevin held. Then, as if on cue, they all started to talk at once. In the babble, Joe heard over and over the words, "The Fréhel treasure!"

"So the story about the treasure was true!" Libby said loudly. "Then what about the ghost? Is that true, too?"

"Hold on!" Kevin shouted. "I never said this is the Fréhel treasure."

Sophie pushed to the front of the crowd. "I do not understand, Kevin," she said. "Where did this come from? How did you find it?"

Everyone grew quiet. They all wanted to hear Kevin's answer.

"Well," he began, "as some of you know, my

mother's ancestors were from Fréhel. I discovered TVI when I came by to explore the village. I went to work for the organization. Then I bought my family's old cottage and started restoring it."

Kevin paused and stared down at the treasure box. Then he said, "One reason was that I wanted to explore my roots. But I had another reason, too. It was a story my mother used to tell me when I was little. A legend about a lost family treasure. It seems one of my ancestors was a servant to the Sieur de Fréhel. He went with him on his adventures around the world. He, too, returned with a fortune."

"I never heard of this," Jean-Claude said.

"No?" Kevin replied. "Well, I guess lords don't pass along stories about their servants. Not the way servants pass along stories about their lords."

"Please go on," Sophie said. "This is fascinating."

"There's not much more to say," Kevin said. "My ancestor was one of the people killed defending the chateau from the gang of bandits. He died without telling anyone where he had hidden his treasure. But even when I was a kid, I just knew it was somewhere inside his house. I was sure he would want it nearby, where he could keep an eye on it. So ever since I bought the cottage, I've been hunting for his hiding place. And this morning, I found it!"

"That's amazing!" Sophie said. "How? Where?"

"Er—the thing is," Kevin said, "I know this guy in Avignon who's a television producer. The last time I saw him, I told him about my treasure hunt. He got very excited. He said it would make a terrific TV show, especially if I found something. But he warned me not to give out any of the details in advance. He'll probably be furious at me for telling you as much as I did."

"We understand," Sophie said.

"What'll you do now?" Marina asked.

Kevin grinned. "Take this box and put it in the bank," he replied. "After that? I'll go on working for TVI and restoring my cottage. And maybe in my spare time, I'll try writing a script for the TV show. Oh—and I plan to contribute a percentage of the treasure to TVI. I figure I owe it."

Everybody clapped and cheered. Kevin waved, tucked the box under his arm, and walked away.

"This has been such a wonderful surprise," Sophie said. "It is hard to think of anything else. But please do not forget we must rehearse for the talent show."

The crowd thinned out. Frank and Joe joined Marie-Laure and Jean-Claude. The twins looked dazed.

"Pretty amazing, isn't it?" Frank observed.

"Very," Jean-Claude said. "When Kevin showed the box of gems, I thought we were looking at the Fréhel treasure. I couldn't understand. The accounts speak of priceless gems in rich settings. That must mean stones that were cut and polished, no?"

"It sounds that way," Frank answered. "But then it

turned out this isn't your ancestor's treasure after all."

"No," Marie-Laure said. She wore a puzzled frown. "Still, I do not understand. Why have we never heard of this other lost treasure? Would that not have made the legend twice as fabulous?"

"I guess Kevin's mom's family kept it secret," Joe suggested. "Maybe they didn't want to set off lots of treasure hunters."

"That must be the answer," Jean-Claude said. He sighed. "I am starting to wish our family had done the same. Excuse me. I am going for a little ride to calm myself."

Jean-Claude walked down the hill.

Sophie bustled over. "He will be back soon, won't he?" she asked, looking after Jean-Claude. "The rehearsal is starting. Marie-Laure, I am placing you at the end of the show. Once you have the children up dancing, they will not want to sit down again. And our karate kids from America will go first."

Frank looked at Joe. He rolled his eyes. What if Sophie introduced them that way the night of the show?

They walked across to the square. Libby was singing a plaintive song about a lady who ran away with a gypsy. She strummed the last chord and smiled.

Welly clapped loudly. "You should lead us in singing one evening," he said. "Why should visitors have all the fun?"

Libby's cheeks turned pink. "Oh, I'm just a beginner, really," she protested. She put her guitar back in its case.

Luis arrived. He had a knapsack over his shoulder and a bright red ball stuck to the end of his nose. He unzipped the knapsack and took out three wooden juggling clubs, a cardboard box, and what looked like a metal propane canister. He put the box and canister aside and picked up the clubs. As he started tossing them rhythmically in the air, people drifted over to watch. Soon there was a solid circle around him.

Now and then Luis reached under his leg or behind his back to catch one of the clubs. The crowd clapped each time. Frank joined in. He thought the juggling was pretty good, but not that unusual.

Then Luis seemed to lose his touch. One club went too high and too far. He ran to catch it. Another came down too far in the other direction. He caught it just before it hit the ground. As he tossed it up again, the third one was coming down somewhere else. Soon he was running madly around the square, trying to catch and throw each club in turn.

The crowd grew silent. Frank crossed his fingers. He did not want to see Luis's humiliation.

Suddenly Luis stopped in the center of the square. He closed his eyes and stretched out his arms in a gesture of despair. *One . . . two . . . three . . .* the clubs smacked down into his open hands. He tucked them under his arm, opened his eyes, and bowed.

When he straightened up, his face was lit by a wide grin.

The spectators cheered wildly. Luis took another bow. When the applause died down, he said, "Thank you, friends. I will not show you my balloon creatures now. I must save my supply of balloons and helium for tomorrow night."

Siri went next. She began to recite a folktale about the elephant and the crocodile. Luis came over and stood next to Frank and Joe.

"That was really terrific," Joe said. "At the end, you had me like totally on edge!"

"That is the idea," Luis said. "The more nervous you become, the more relieved you are when it turns out okay."

"So you use helium in your balloon animals?" Frank asked. "That's unusual, isn't it?"

"Oh, yes," Luis agreed. "And I do not use much. Just enough to make them seem to weigh nothing. It would not be good if I made some child a dachshund and it floated away!"

Jean-Claude returned just as Siri finished. He whistled two songs and imitated some birdcalls. The birds must have been French. Frank didn't recognize their names. He couldn't tell if Jean-Claude's imitations were realistic or not, but they did sound pretty much like birds.

"Marie-Laure?" Sophie called. "We are not going in order, but if you—"

"I am sorry," Marie-Laure replied. "I have not had time to make a tape of the music. I promise to get it done before the show."

That meant it was time for Frank and Joe. They walked through a demonstration of tae kwon do. "Tomorrow night we'll do the movements full out," Frank explained, when they finished. "This was just to give you the flavor."

The bell rang for lunch. Frank and Joe found themselves at one end of the table with Welly, Luis, and Libby. Gert came in and sat down near them. The conversation turned to people's plans after high school.

"We have good universities in South Africa," Welly said. "Even so, I would like to go to Oxford. I have read so much about it. Luis, what of you? Will you stay in Argentina?"

"I don't know," Luis replied. "I just learned that there is a national academy for clowning and circus arts near Paris. I want to visit it before I go home."

"All this education is a waste of time," Gert said. "You will learn much more if you go into the real world and get a real job. If I had wasted my time at the university . . ."

"I could not disagree more," Libby said. "My older sister went into advertising after she left school. She did very well, too. But last year, she gave up her position to read for a university degree full-time. She says she only regrets she didn't do it straightaway."

"Joe? Frank?" Welly said. "What about you?"

"Just about all the kids we know plan to go to college," Frank said. "So do we. But first, we have to get through high school. Right now it seems like it'll never end!"

The others laughed.

By the time the cheese course came, the bread basket was empty. Frank looked along the table. The others were empty, too. No bread anywhere.

"I'll get more," Jean-Claude offered. He gathered three of the empty baskets and went down the stairs to the kitchen. A minute later, he returned. The baskets were still empty.

"We face a *crise*," he announced. "The truck of the baker did not arrive today. We have no bread for dinner."

"No big deal," Joe said. "For one meal, we can go without."

"Impossible!" Marie-Laure said. "Barbarous! How can one eat without a piece of bread to hold in the hand!"

"There is a solution," Jean-Claude said. "After lunch, I will ride to the *boulangerie* in St. Sernin. I will bring back a dozen baguettes. And by breakfast tomorrow, the truck of the baker will no doubt be fixed."

"You don't need to do that," Gert said. "Kevin can go in the van after he gets back."

"Bicycles are friendlier to the environment," Jean-

Claude replied. "And besides, it will be healthy exercise."

The others at the table laughed. All of them were getting more than enough exercise every day. The work they did guaranteed that.

The schedule for the pétanque tournament was posted on the bulletin board outside Sophie's office. Once lunch was over, Frank, Joe, and the others wandered down to check it.

Jean-Claude arrived with a helmet on his head and a long canvas bag slung over his shoulder. He took one of the bikes from the rack and swung onto the saddle. "The baguette express is now leaving on track four," he cracked. "I'll be back soon."

He started to ride onto the steep path to the parking area.

"Jean-Claude, stop," Gert called. "Wait a moment. I want to ask a favor."

Jean-Claude squeezed the bike's hand brakes. Frank saw a look of alarm cross his face. He pressed both brake handles all the way against the hand grips. They did nothing at all. The brakes were not working. The cables must have snapped.

The path grew steeper. The bicycle picked up speed. A terrible crash was only moments away!

11 Getting the Brakes

The runaway bike began to roll faster. Jean-Claude clutched the handlebars and steered around the rocks that dotted the path. On one side the ground fell steeply. The other was an upward slope of rough stone.

"Jean-Claude, jump!" Joe shouted. He broke into a run, Frank right behind him.

The French teen crouched over the handlebars. He seemed paralyzed by the danger he faced.

"Jump!" Joe repeated. Frank shouted, too.

Jean-Claude suddenly straightened up. With a powerful twist of his arms, he aimed the front wheel of the bike at a solitary bush beside the path. The wheel snagged the branches. The rear part of the bike flipped up. Jean-Claude was thrown forward.

He instantly tucked himself into a ball. A moment later he landed hard on his back.

Joe and Frank were the first to reach Jean-Claude. "Take it easy," Joe urged. "Stay where you are while we get help."

Jean-Claude struggled to sit up. "I am all right," he insisted. "I need a moment to catch my breath, that's all."

Marie-Laure ran down the path and knelt in the dirt next to her brother. She took his arm and spoke in rapid French. Her voice was full of concern.

Jean-Claude replied reassuringly. He pushed himself up onto his feet and rubbed his back. "Ouf!" he said. "I will have some blues tomorrow for sure."

"Blacks and blues, he means," Marie-Laure explained.

"What happened?" Joe asked. "How did you lose control that way?"

Everybody in the vicinity was crowding down the path. They listened to hear Jean-Claude's answer.

"I don't know," Jean-Claude said. "The brakes would not work."

Frank picked up the bicycle. The rim of the front wheel was bent from the crash. He leaned close to peer at the front brake. Then he did the same with the rear brake.

"Look at this," he said in a steely voice. Joe, Marie-Laure, and Jean-Claude joined him. Frank pointed to the nut that held the front brake cable in place. It was loose enough to turn by hand. "The rear brake is the same," Frank added.

"I don't understand," Jean-Claude said. "The brakes worked as they should when I rode just before lunch. How could this happen?"

Frank looked over his shoulder at the circle of listeners. Lowering his voice, he said, "I don't think this was an accident. Someone must have deliberately loosened those nuts."

Marie-Laure turned pale. "You could have been injured for life," she told Jean-Claude. "This cannot be tolerated. We must stop this madness before it is too late!"

"To stop it, we must learn who is responsible," Jean-Claude pointed out. He gave Joe and Frank a hopeful look.

"We'll do what we can," Joe promised. "You say you used the bike before lunch?"

Jean-Claude nodded. "Yes, and everything was as it should be. Then I left the bicycle in the rack as usual and came to the rehearsal in the square. You recall. You were all there."

"Then we all went in to lunch," Frank said slowly. "And after lunch we gathered at the office, right next to the bike rack. By then your brakes had been tampered with."

"That means the tampering must have been done while we were at lunch," Joe said. "But how can that be? We were all together."

"Some stranger could have crept up and done it," Marie-Laure suggested.

"A stranger could not have known which was my bicycle," Jean-Claude retorted.

"Maybe he didn't care," Joe said. "What if he simply fiddled with the first bike he came to?"

"Or with more than one," Frank added. "We'd better check all the others before anyone goes riding."

The van pulled into the parking area and stopped. Kevin got out. He saw them gathered on the path and hastened up to join them. "What's wrong?" he asked urgently. "Is something the matter?"

Jean-Claude explained.

As Kevin listened, his expression became more and more grim. At last he exploded. "Enough is enough! I'm going to find out who's doing this. And when I do, they're going to be very sorry!"

He scowled at the crowd of onlookers. "Please come with me to the office," he said sternly. "I need to have a talk with all of you, one by one."

The teens glanced at one another nervously. When Kevin strode up the path, they hesitated, then straggled after him. Marie-Laure put an arm around Jean-Claude's waist and helped him to walk. Frank hoisted the damaged bike onto his shoulder.

"Too bad we can't eavesdrop on these 'talks' of Kevin's," Joe said in an undertone. "Hmm . . . you don't think—"

"Not an option," Frank said crisply. "If he caught

us, we'd be on a train to Paris before sundown."

The Hardys walked up the path and joined the crowd outside the office. During the wait, Frank checked the brakes on the other bikes in the rack. He asked Luis and Libby to come watch what he did. There was no point in fueling whatever suspicions Kevin might have.

As far as Frank could tell, there was nothing wrong with the other bikes. The saboteur had chosen Jean-Claude's bike either on purpose or by chance.

Manu came out of the office. "Libby?" he said. "You're next."

"How was it?" Antonio asked as Libby went inside.

Manu shrugged. "I told him I have done nothing wrong," he said. "Did he believe me? Who knows? He is very angry."

"I feel sick," Siri said. She held her hand to her waist.

"Go lie down," Marie-Laure told her. "I'll explain to Kevin."

"Will he listen to you?" Siri asked doubtfully.

Marie-Laure looked grim. "I think he had better," she said. "My brother could have been killed. Surely Kevin will not suspect *me!*"

"He might," Frank said. "He might wonder if Jean-Claude knew ahead of time the brakes were rigged to fail. Jean-Claude could have staged the whole incident himself . . . or with your help."

Marie-Laure stared at him in disbelief. "You dare!"

she blazed. "After we worked so hard to be your friends! I will never speak to you again!"

She rushed away in tears. Jean-Claude gave Frank a hostile look and hurried after her.

"Way to go, Frank," Joe growled. "You're a real diplomat."

"Hold on!" Frank protested. "I didn't say *I* believed it, just that Kevin *might*. Though if you look at the timing, Jean-Claude had more opportunity to monkey with the brakes than the rest of us. I can't quite get with the sinister stranger theory. Too noticeable in a tiny, remote place like Fréhel."

"There's such a thing as being too suspicious," Joe said.

The afternoon dragged on. At the end only Joe and Frank were left. Kevin called them in together. He had a pad full of notes on the desk in front of him.

"As far as I'm concerned, you guys are in the clear," he said. "This sabotage started before you got here. But I have to ask you. Have you noticed anything out of the ordinary? Anything that might tell us who's responsible for these incidents?"

Joe looked over at Frank. Was this the time to share what they had learned with Kevin? He was second in command of TVI. He had a right to know. But what could they tell him, really? That one of the teens might be working for Immo-Trust? Without a name and evidence to back it up, that wouldn't do Kevin any good. It might even point a finger at an innocent person. Better to wait until their case was more complete.

"Sorry," Joe said. "Afraid not."

"Same here," Frank said. "But we'll be on the lookout."

"I'd appreciate that," Kevin said. "Okay, then. You can go."

Dinner was pretty grim. Marie-Laure acted as if Joe and Frank didn't exist. It was the same later, when everyone walked up to the ridge to watch the sunset.

Joe looked for a chance to go over to Jean-Claude. "This feud is really dumb," he said. "Frank didn't mean anything by what he said."

"I know that," Jean-Claude replied. "But my sister is very upset by all that has happened. She does not know at whom she should be upset. The result, she is upset at Frank. Give her time. She will realize she is being unfair."

"I hope so," Joe said. "We need to pull together. Unless we solve this case quickly, someone else may get hurt, worse than you did."

At breakfast Sophie announced, "Because of the disruption yesterday, the pétanque tournament will resume at five this afternoon. The playoffs will be tomorrow."

"That does not give much time to practice," Antonio complained.

"So what?" Welly said. "The way we play, practice won't help much anyway."

Sophie pretended not to hear. "And as you know," she continued, "this morning we visit Peyrane and its world-famous ocher mines. Be at the parking area in twenty minutes."

"What's an ocher mine?" Frank murmured to Marina.

"A place where people dig up ocher," she replied. "You'll see. It is quite remarkable."

This time Frank and Joe rode in the van with Kevin. The Fréhels started to get in, too. Then Marie-Laure saw Frank. She spun on her heel and went over to the old Citroën. With an apologetic look, Jean-Claude followed her.

Joe noticed the van's mileage counter. It read 9976 km. "How long a trip is this?" he asked Kevin.

"Peyrane? Not far," Kevin replied. "Fifteen or twenty kilometers."

Joe sat back, satisfied. So they might be able to watch the counter roll over from 9999 to 10000. Cool!

Once down from the ridge, they drove along narrow roads lined with fields of grapevines. After a few minutes, the countryside became more rolling. Ahead Joe saw a new range of hills covered with dense brush and scrub trees. He glanced out at the shoulder of the road.

"Hey, guys, look," he said. "The dirt here is bright yellow!"

110

"Just wait," Kevin said. They rounded a curve and topped a rise.

Joe felt his jaw drop. Ahead was an entire cliff colored dark orange. Beyond it, another was bloodred. The landscape looked like a spectacular sunset.

"What you're looking at is called ocher," Kevin explained. "It's a natural mineral. You mix it with paint to get different colors."

"Oh, sure," Frank said. "I've seen the name on tubes of oil paints. Yellow ocher."

"Right," Kevin said. "If you go back a hundred years, paints all over the world were colored with ocher from these hills. Then somebody invented a cheaper synthetic substitute. That was the end for the ocher mines of Peyrane."

Kevin turned off into a parking area. The Citroën was close behind them. They parked by a big wooden sign that read "Active Ocher Mill—1892" in several languages.

"This place is interesting," Kevin said. "Then there's a path along the cliffs from here into town. You'll have time in Peyrane for lunch and a look around the town."

"Aren't you coming?" Libby asked.

Kevin shook his head. "I have to run some errands on the other side of the valley. I'll come back later to pick you up."

The tour of the ocher mill did not take long. Most of the teens were not that interested. While Joe watched the big mechanical hammers that pounded the ocher into fine granules, the rest of the group started up the trail.

"Come on," Frank urged. "Let's catch up."

Joe took the lead. The rough path followed the edge of the cliff. Through gaps in the bushes they could see across a narrow valley to other cliffs striped in shades of yellow, orange, and red.

Joe was turning to point out a view to Frank when the ground gave way under his feet. Startled, he grabbed the nearest bush with both hands. A moment later he was dangling over a sheer fifty-foot drop.

12 Deadly Diversion

"Joe!" Frank shouted. "Hold on!"

"I will," Joe gasped. "But hurry!"

Frank flung himself to the ground and crawled toward the edge of the cliff. As he went, he tested the ground in front of him with his hand. If he, too, slipped over the cliff, there would be no hope for either of them.

As he drew closer, Frank took a hasty look at the bush Joe was clinging to. He could see its roots. The strain of Joe's weight was gradually pulling them up from the thin soil. How much longer would they hold? A minute? Less?

"Don't worry," Frank called. "I'm coming!"

"Good thing," Joe said faintly. "I forgot my parachute."

Frank was almost close enough to grasp Joe's arms. But if he did, what would stop both of them from sliding over the edge? He pushed himself up on his elbows and looked around. A few feet to his left was a small, gnarled tree. He rolled toward it. Clasping the trunk between his calves, he crossed his feet at the ankles to lock the grip. Then he reached again for Joe.

No good! His grip on the tree held him too far back to reach Joe's arms. He needed to be about five inches closer. It didn't sound like much, five inches. But if he couldn't close the gap, it was as bad as five miles.

"Frank?" Joe said in a strained voice. "I think I'm slipping."

"Hold on!" Frank repeated. No time for half measures. He unhooked his ankles and slid forward. He left only the toes of his right foot tucked in back of the tree trunk. Stretching to the limit, he reached forward and touched Joe's wrists. He closed his fingers around them with all the force he had.

"Okay, get ready to let go and grab my wrists," Frank shouted. "On three . . . one . . . two . . . *three!*"

All of Joe's weight was suddenly pulling at Frank's arms. He heard a pop in his left shoulder. A moment later he felt it, too. He blocked off that part of his mind and concentrated on pulling Joe up.

Everything worked together—arms, abs, thighs, even the muscles in his shin that kept the right foot's grip on the tree. Slowly, he moved back from the edge, pulling Joe with him.

Soon Joe's upper body was on level ground. He twisted to the right and got his foot and knee up on the cliff edge. Frank gave an extra hard tug. Joe flung himself into a roll that took him well away from the drop. He lay on his back, his chest heaving from the strain.

"Whew!" Frank said, once he had caught his breath. His shoulder ached. "How did you miss the path?"

"I didn't," Joe gasped. "The path leads straight over the edge."

Frank sat up and looked around. Joe was right. "I wonder how the others missed falling the way you did," he said. He stood up and followed the path back the way they had come.

About twenty feet back, he noticed a second path forking off. A broken tree limb blocked it. He touched the broken end. It was still damp with sap. As he scanned the underbrush, he noticed a flash of white. It was a wooden sign on a stake with big red letters that Frank assumed warned people not to go on the path he and Joe had taken.

Joe joined him. "So that's it," he said. "Somebody blocked the right path, then took the warning sign off the dangerous one. Another booby trap, even more deadly than the others."

"Deadly . . . and personal," Frank said. "This must

have been rigged *after* the rest of the group went by. It was aimed directly at us!"

Joe helped Frank replace the sign. Then they strode quickly along the real path. Ten minutes later they caught up to the group. Marina heard them and looked back. She burst out laughing. The others looked and started laughing, too.

"What have you two been doing?" Welly asked.

"Gathering local color!" Libby gasped out. She laughed so hard she had to hold her sides.

Frank looked at Joe, then down at himself. The ocher dirt had dyed their clothes and skin bright orange.

"We took a fall," he said.

"You mean a dirt bath," Luis said.

Sophie stepped forward. "I'll arrange for showers and clean clothes in Peyrane," she said. "I'm afraid what you're wearing may be ruined. Ocher stains are very hard to get out."

"That's for sure," Siri said. "On our first visit, I got ocher on a pair of white socks. They're still orange."

"Have all of you been here before, then?" Frank asked.

Most of them nodded. Valentina said, "Not I. I was not feeling well the last time."

Frank's heart sank. He had hoped to eliminate some of the teens as suspects. Whoever set the trap had to know about the treacherous path. But that could be any of them except Valentina.

"When we were trying to catch up," he said, "I thought I saw somebody up ahead and heard a voice call us. Was it one of you? Or were you together the whole time?"

"It couldn't have been one of us," Marina said. "We were together the whole time. Oh—except when Marie-Laure stayed back to tie her shoelace. But she was just away a couple of minutes."

Frank looked at Joe. Marie-Laure had made no secret of being angry with them. Angry enough to set a dangerous trap?

If so, did that mean she was behind the other dirty tricks? No, that was impossible. She wouldn't have risked tampering with her brother's brakes. Unless . . . what if Marie-Laure and Jean-Claude had staged the whole bike incident to throw off any suspicion of them?

"We need to talk," Frank muttered to Joe.

"I agree," Joe muttered back. "Soon."

A five-minute walk brought the group to Peyrane. The town was built around the upper slopes of a hill. The stone houses were clustered so close together that their orange tile roofs seemed joined into one huge ripply surface. From window ledges, doorsteps, and balcony railings, pots of bright red geraniums cheered the scene.

While the others looked around a curio shop, Sophie took Frank and Joe to a small inn. The manager agreed to let them use his shower room.

"Listen," Joe said, once they were alone. "I know what you're thinking. It even makes a screwy kind of sense. But I don't believe it for a moment."

"I don't *want* to believe it," Frank replied. "I like Marie-Laure and Jean-Claude. But face it, whoever rigged that trap had a very small window of opportunity. Five or ten minutes max. And it sounds as if she is the only one in the group who could have taken advantage of it."

"Hold it," Joe said. "Let's say she's the only one who left the group. Okay. But on a narrow trail, you go single file. Somebody has to be the caboose. Who'll notice if you fall back a little? And how long do you need to pull up the warning sign, then break off a tree limb and put it across the path?"

"I see your point," Frank said. He stepped into the shower. Over the noise of the water, he added, "We should try to find out who the caboose was. But I'm still going to keep a sharp eye on Marie-Laure."

Sophie returned with T-shirts and drawstring pants for them. The T-shirts featured a garish painting of Peyrane's ocher cliffs and the pants felt like pajamas, but neither Frank nor Joe was in the mood to complain. They rejoined the group. When Luis teased them about their new garb, they took it with good humor.

"We'll have lunch first, then tour the town," Sophie announced. She led them up a stone-paved street and into a low, narrow café. Frank saw only a few small tables inside. Where were they going to sit?

Sophie waved to the apron-clad man behind the bar and walked through the café. On the other side of a small back room, a door led outside. At the foot of a set of stone steps was a garden. The view extended across the rooftops of the town to the ocher cliffs. An arbor covered with grapevines shaded a long table already set for lunch.

Joe sidled up to Frank. In a low voice, he said, "According to Gert, Libby was the last in line. He says she held up the group by dawdling."

"I'll check it out," Frank replied.

Libby was on the other side of the table. The seat next to her was free. Frank went over and sat down.

The first course was cut-up fresh vegetables with a spicy mayonnaise. Between bites, Frank and Libby talked about how unusual Peyrane was.

"Oh, and look what I bought," Libby said. From her shoulder bag, she pulled out a boxed set of small bottles filled with different shades of ocher. "It's for a friend in London who's an art student. Don't you think she'll be thrilled with it?"

"Bound to be," Frank replied. "That was a spectacular trail we hiked in on, wasn't it? A little narrow, though. If you're at the back of the line, you don't see that much."

Libby looked him up and down. "I shouldn't have thought it was a problem for *you*," she said. "You and

Joe are so tall. But I certainly know about that. I generally try to be near the front."

"Not today?" Frank asked casually.

"No," Libby said. "Siri and I got to chatting and fell back a bit. When we realized, we had to move quite briskly to catch up with the others. I'm afraid some of them were rather cross with us."

Frank thought this over. Libby and Siri had been together at the back of the line. Neither of them could have set the trap without the other's noticing. So Marie-Laure was chief suspect again. Unless Libby and Siri were both involved . . . ?

Frank shook his head. If he didn't watch it, he would start to suspect *everyone*!

After lunch the teens wandered through the winding streets of the town.

"Oh, look," Marina said. She pointed into a narrow gap between two houses. A long flight of steps led upward. A small sign read, "Église—Church," with an arrow. "Let's climb to the top. The view must be marvelous."

Frank suddenly realized he did not have the plastic bag with his ocher-stained jeans and shirt. He recalled setting it on the ground next to his chair at lunch. It must still be there.

"I have to go back," he told Joe. "I'll catch up with you later."

Frank knew the café was lower down and to the right from where they were. It would be a waste of time to backtrack along the meandering route the group had followed through town. Frank took the first street that led downhill through the tightly packed houses.

After a few blocks, the street Frank was on emptied into a wide, bright boulevard. On one side was a solid row of three-story buildings painted in different shades of red, yellow, and orange. The other side looked out across the valley. Frank waited for a few cars to pass. Then he walked across to the opposite sidewalk.

The ground dropped away steeply. Twenty-five feet below the level of the street was a grassy park dotted with trees, whose top branches were just five feet below Frank. A low wrought iron fence kept pedestrians from straying over the edge.

Frank was enjoying the view when he heard the high whine of a car engine at full throttle. He looked around. A blue sedan was accelerating in his direction. Thirty feet away, it swerved and jumped the curb onto the sidewalk.

As the car hurtled straight at Frank, he caught one quick glimpse of the driver. His face was completely hidden behind a black ski mask.

13 Monsieur Tarzan

The blue sedan picked up speed as it darted along the sidewalk. Frank cast one urgent glance around. No time to dash out of the car's path. Nothing solid to find shelter behind. No chance to escape being run down . . . except one very long shot.

Frank took a deep breath and jumped up onto the top rail of the iron fence. For one split second he balanced there. Then he crouched down like a sprinter on the starting blocks. Arms spread to their widest, he flung himself down toward the upper branches of the nearest tree.

He was still in the air when he heard the grating screech of metal scraping metal. In the distance a horn blared and someone started shouting.

Frank struck the canopy of leaves and branches feet

first. In a flash, he wrapped his left arm around his head to protect his eyes. One sharp twig ripped his new T-shirt. Another left a long scratch on his right arm. Then his fall stopped, and he found himself straddling a thin branch that dipped and swayed with his weight. It felt as if it might break at any moment.

"Eh bien, Monsieur Tarzan," an angry voice shouted. *"Vous faites quoi là, déjà!"*

Frank took a cautious look in the direction of the ground. A middle-aged man wearing blue work clothes and carrying a rake glared up at him. Frank didn't catch all his words. He didn't need to. The accusing finger that gestured downward got the message across.

"I'm coming down," Frank called back. To himself, he added, But not too fast, I hope!

Carefully, he inched along the limb toward the trunk of the tree. Once there, he climbed down until he was six feet or so from the ground. Then he let himself drop the rest of the way.

The man with the rake was waiting at the base of the tree. He let loose a volley of rapid-fire French, illustrated with an amazing assortment of gestures.

"Look, I'm sorry," Frank said. He threw in an apologetic smile and a shrug of his shoulders. "It was a matter of life or death. *Vie* or *morte!*"

The workman was not impressed. With a broad sweep of his arm, he pointed toward a nearby park gate. To punctuate the sentence, he stamped his foot.

Frank left. His knee hurt and the scratch on his arm stung, but he knew how lucky he was. That was no prank he had just survived. Whoever was hiding behind that ski mask had meant to kill him!

The street that bordered the park made a wide loop and joined the boulevard. Frank went up the hill and got his bearings. A hundred yards to his right, he saw a crowd gathered around a familiar-looking blue car. He hurried over.

A bearded man in a brown suit was talking heatedly to a uniformed police officer. From time to time, he pointed at the front fender of the car, which was badly dented and scraped, then appealed to the crowd. The officer nodded and took notes.

Frank was positive this was the car that had tried to run him over. "Excuse me," he said. "Do any of you speak English?"

A young woman in a light summer dress eyed Frank's torn T-shirt and scratched arm. She said, "I do. Is something wrong?"

Frank quickly explained what had happened. When she translated his words to the officer, everyone started talking at once.

The officer held up a hand for silence. Then he spoke to the young woman. "He asks, where and when is this event?" she translated.

"Over there, just a few minutes ago," Frank told her. Moments later Frank, the officer, and the man in the brown suit were striding down the sidewalk.

The young woman, who introduced herself as Mireille, came along to translate.

Frank easily found the spot. He pointed out the streaks of blue paint on the iron railing. Down below, the guy with the rake watched dubiously. He made his way up, and he and the officer exchanged a couple of sentences, accompanied by gestures.

"You are to please come to the gendarmerie," Mireille told Frank, after another burst of French. "It is about a formal report of the incident."

"Okay," Frank said. "But my friends must be wondering where I am. They'll be worried."

"It will not be long," Mireille promised.

The police station was a new building surrounded by a high wall. Four or five blue station wagons with red lights on their roofs were parked in the courtyard. The officer took Frank and Mireille inside and led them to a small, cluttered office. He inserted a form in a battered typewriter.

"Passeport," he said. Frank handed it over. After he copied the details, the officer gave it back.

The interview stretched out. The officer asked a question. Mireille translated it to Frank, then translated his answer to the officer. The officer typed slowly, with two fingers, then asked another question.

After twenty minutes Frank wondered what would happen if he stood up and walked out. Suddenly, from the outer office, he heard a familiar voice say,

"Can you please tell them my brother's missing?"

"Hey, Joe!" Frank called. "In here!"

Frank spent most of the ride back to Fréhel explaining what had happened to him. Everyone had a different reaction to the story.

"I wish I could have seen you leap into the tree," Libby said. "You must have been a picture!"

"That makes two shirts you have ruined today," Siri said.

"These French," Gert said. "They cannot be trusted with anything on wheels."

"Oh, come!" Manu protested. "That is unfair."

Gert scowled at him. "It is not. Cars, trucks, motorcycles—no matter. I went once to Paris with my high school class. The pollution that week was very bad. The government had barred all motor vehicles from the city. Yet my friend was knocked over and injured by an idiot on roller skates. Anything on wheels, I tell you!"

Manu gave him a quizzical look but didn't respond. Kevin bumped up the track to the parking area and stopped next to the path. "Terminus Fréhel," he said in a train announcer's voice. "All out."

Frank and Joe were the last to start up the path. This was their first chance to talk privately since the police station.

"You're sure the whole group was together the whole time?" Frank asked.

126

"Positive," Joe answered. "I had them in sight every minute, right up until I went off to look for you. Whoever the guy in the ski mask was, he's not one of our bunch."

"Which leaves Immo-Trust," Frank said. "How about this? Their inside guy passes the word about our excursion today. One of their other people goes to Peyrane and shadows us."

"And steals a car off the street and tries to kill you with it?" Joe said. "I don't think real estate developers get that kind of training."

Frank pounded his palm with his fist. "I know it sounds nutty," he said. "But *somebody* did it!"

"Hmmm . . . what are the odds two different people tried to harm us the same day?" Joe asked.

"Meaning what?" Frank replied.

"Just this," Joe replied. "I know Marie-Laure wasn't driving that car. And now I don't believe she tried to send us over that cliff, either."

"I don't want to believe it," Frank said. "But we're very short on good candidates."

Jean-Claude was waiting at the top of the path. "Frank, go wash and dress, quickly," he said. "Our match begins in fifteen minutes."

For a moment Frank was baffled. Then he remembered. The pétanque tournament!

"Look, can't you get someone else?" he pleaded. "I've had a hard day."

"The teams were chosen at random," Jean-Claude

reminded him. "It would not be fair to change them now. You will have fun. I guarantee it!"

An hour later Frank had to agree. The game *was* fun. He even managed to place some of his balls within scoring distance of the target. It helped, of course, that Jean-Claude was a good player. Their opponents, Gert and Antonio, both played fairly well, too, so the match was not a walkover.

At the end Jean-Claude said, "Tomorrow will be interesting. A real family affair, eh?"

"How's that?" Frank asked.

"The semifinal. We are down to play Joe and Marie-Laure," Jean-Claude explained.

"Er—do you think they'll still play together?" Frank asked. "After all . . ."

Jean-Claude waved his hand. "*Bof!* That is all in the past," he said. "Done and forgotten."

Frank wondered if Joe knew it was all in the past. Or was he expected simply to guess?

Just before seven o'clock, the bus from the *colonie* lurched up the track from the valley and parked. The kids filed off and ran up the path, shouting and laughing. They ranged in age from about eight to twelve. All were wearing blue shorts, yellow T-shirts, and white sailor caps with the brims turned down for shade.

A charcoal grill had been set up in front of the community center. The tangy smell of cooking sausage wafted down the street. Frank's mouth began to water.

Joe joined him. "I got a tip from Manu," he said. "There are two kinds of sausage on the grill. Watch out for the one called merguez. Sometimes it's spicy enough to send you into orbit."

"Thanks," Frank said. "Hey, did you hear? We're playing each other at pétanque tomorrow."

"I know," Joe said. "Marie-Laure told me. She made like I'm her old friend and partner. I didn't say anything about the way she acted earlier. It felt rude."

"I think that was supposed to count as an apology," Frank said. "Take it or leave it."

Sophie brought the kids back from a tour of the village. They lined up for a picnic of sausages, buns, and potato chips. Frank, Joe, and the rest of the TVI bunch fell in behind them. Soon they were all sitting around the square, eating and talking.

After sunset the talent show started. Siri got a last-minute attack of nerves and refused to go on. Sophie quickly rearranged the order. The kids seemed to like Libby's folk songs, even though they were in English. And some of them already knew how to do the local folk dance Marie-Laure led.

When it was time for the Hardys to do their martial arts demonstration, Joe murmured, "Let's make this good."

"You got it, dude," Frank replied.

It *was* good. Both of them put a lot of energy into their leaps and kicks. The kids in the audience gasped when Joe's leg grazed the side of Frank's head. They screamed when Frank did a hip throw that left Joe sprawling in the dirt. And they stood up and cheered when, after a lightning series of holds, the brothers jumped to their feet and bowed.

Frank and Joe grinned and went to sit down next to Welly. The finale was Luis and his clown act. But where was he?

Suddenly a figure dressed all in white did a cartwheel into the center of the circle and began to juggle. Instead of clubs, he used clear plastic bottles with chemical glowsticks inside. Red, yellow, and green fire spun into the night sky in dizzying patterns, accompanied by the oohs and aahs of the kids.

After the juggling, Luis began to twist helium balloons into stars, hats, crowns, and a dozen different animals. He tucked smaller glowsticks into the balloons, too. By the time he was done, the thrilled smiles on the kids' faces were lit by the eerie glow from their own personal balloons.

At last it was time for the children to leave. From the village, the TVI volunteers watched the dots of colored fire bob down the path to the waiting bus.

"That was beautiful," Libby said with a sigh.

No one had anything to add.

* * *

That night Frank had another dream. He was with the others on the ridge. A spectral figure floated past the windows of the chateau. No, he was in the square. Luis twisted a glowing helium balloon into the shape of a person.

Luis looked up and met Frank's eyes. With a deliberate gesture, he twisted the neck of the balloon figure. The head came off in his hand. He let it go. Glowing an eerie green, the detached head floated slowly up, past the trees, into blackness.

Frank opened his eyes and stared at the ceiling. So *that* was it!

14 Breakfast Battle

Early the next morning Frank got up and touched Joe's shoulder. "Let's go for a walk," he whispered.

The sun was just peeping over the horizon when they left the house. They walked up to the ridge and sat down on a flat rock that overlooked the valley. First Frank spoke while Joe listened. Then the conversation became more equal. Finally they stood up and walked back to the village.

They found Luis alone in the room. He was just getting dressed. "Aha, the early birds," he said. "You put on quite a show last night. I must remember never to get into a fight with one of you."

"Your act was really something, too," Joe said. "The kids loved it. And so did we."

"It gave me an idea," Frank said. He walked over to the window and gazed out at the chateau. "What if I took one of those glowsticks and put it in a big balloon, then filled it with helium?"

"How original!" Luis said, in an ironic tone. "I must have done that twenty times last night."

"Sure," Frank replied. "But here's the twist. I put a string on the balloon and tie it down somewhere out of sight. And I put something that burns very slowly next to the string."

"Interesting," Luis said. "But what is the point?"

"When the fire reaches the string, the balloon rises and flies away," Joe said. "And if it's dark out, people see this weird glowing thing that appears out of nowhere and then vanishes into the sky. Neat, huh?"

"Of course," Frank said, "you'd want it to rise very slowly. You'd have to put just the right amount of helium in. That would take a lot of know-how and experience."

"Certainly it would," Luis said with a smile.

Frank exchanged a look with Joe. He said, "You admit it, then? You created that floating glow that scared everybody the other day?"

"Of course," Luis said, still smiling. "It was very effective, wasn't it? Setting is everything."

"Wait a minute," Joe said. "You admit that you've been trying to make people think Fréhel is haunted? You've been trying to wreck TVI?"

The smile vanished. "What?" Luis said. "Wreck TVI? Nothing of the sort. It was only to tease you, the newcomers. What is that word? A hazing."

"And the stone that fell from the chateau?" Frank said. "Was that just hazing? Somebody could have been hurt."

"I know nothing about that," Luis protested. "I created the floating spirit, and I made the moans to be heard during the mistral. That is all."

"What about Jean-Claude's bicycle?" Joe demanded. "Who loosened the brakes?"

"I have no idea," Luis said. He was starting to look alarmed.

"Were you working with anybody else?" Joe continued. "Welly, for example?"

"Maybe Welly suspected," Luis replied. "He knew I borrowed his tape machine. But he did nothing he shouldn't."

"And no one else worked with you or encouraged you?" Frank probed.

"I have no more to say," Luis told him.

"That means yes," Frank told Joe. To Luis, he said, "We'll have to tell Sophie about this, you know. Unless you want to tell her yourself."

Luis stared past Frank at the window. After a moment he said, "Yes, I do. Thank you."

"We'll say nothing to anyone," Frank promised. "And we'd like you to do the same."

"I promise," Luis said.

Just then Welly bounded up the stairs with a towel draped around his neck. "Rise and shine!" he said. "Time for the most important meal of the day!"

On the way to breakfast, Luis walked ahead. Frank and Joe watched him go up to Sophie and speak earnestly. The two crossed to the square and sat down.

At breakfast the conversation was about the show the night before. "Those kids were so cute," Libby declared. "I could have hugged them all!"

"I was very interested by what Joe and Frank did," Narguib said. "Was that karate?"

"Not exactly," Joe told him. "More like a variation on tae kwon do, seasoned with a few kung fu moves."

"Luis juggles beautifully," Siri said. "And those sticks that glow in different colors are amazing. I wonder what is in them."

"Chemicals," Welly said. "I should think they cause pollution. Most new gadgets do."

"That reminds me," Manu said. "Gert, didn't you tell us you were in Paris once when they banned cars because of pollution?"

Gert eyed him warily. "Yes. It was an excursion of my high school class. Why?"

"This spring I did a term project on controlling pollution emergencies," Manu said. "The only time I think they banned cars in Paris was seven years ago. But you weren't in high school seven years ago. You would have been far too young."

135

"Your research was faulty," Gert growled. "Perhaps they did not ban all cars, only some. What does it matter?"

"Oh, it doesn't," Manu said hastily. "I was curious, that's all."

Frank found that he was curious, too. Hadn't Gert said something once about having taken a job *after* high school, instead of attending university?

"Hey, Gert," Frank said. "How old are you?"

"I will be eighteen my next birthday," Gert replied.

"Oh? Cool. When's that?" Frank continued.

"The eleventh of October," Gert told him.

"And what year were you born?" Frank asked quickly.

"In nineteen eighty—I mean . . . " Gert glared at Frank and fell silent.

"It's hard to do subtraction under pressure, isn't it," Frank said. "But most people know their birth year by heart. Why don't you check your identity card? It's on that, isn't it? May I look?"

Gert's hand went to his hip pocket. "Certainly not," he said. "What business is this of yours?"

"I'm wondering if you're who you pretend to be," Frank said. "Someone at TVI is here under false colors. If it isn't you, why not show me your ID?"

From the doorway, Sophie said, "Or if you prefer, Gert, you may show me. You said you would bring it by the office two weeks ago."

"Very well," Gert said defiantly. He pulled a

leather folder from his pocket and tossed it on the table near Frank. "You are right. I am not eighteen. I am twenty-three. I pretended to be younger. I wanted to come to TVI, and it is open only to high school students."

"If you had explained, we might have found a way," Sophie said.

"It's a good thing you didn't," Frank said. He had just opened Gert's ID folder and noticed a business card tucked behind his identity card. It indicated that Gert Hochsmer was a senior trainee at the Paris branch of Immo-Trust.

"You—" Jean-Claude shouted. "You are one of the people who are trying to destroy my heritage!"

Gert gave a snort. "Who cares about worn-out aristocrats like you? The people who have money *now* are the ones who count. If they want to pay good money for this pile of old rocks, they should be able to!"

"Speaking of rocks," Joe said. "You rigged the booby traps? The stone that rolled onto the road, the one that fell from the wall? Those were clever."

"Yes, weren't they?" Gert replied. "They took much thought. And much thought to make sure they injured no one. I am not a barbarian."

"I disagree," Marie-Laure said softly.

"What about Jean-Claude's brakes?" Frank said. "He was almost hurt badly."

"That was difficult," Gert said. "I expected he would take his usual ride along the ridge. When I saw him start down the path, I called out to stop him. I did not want him hurt, only frightened."

"Fooey!" Joe exploded. "What about trying to run over my brother? You think he wouldn't have been hurt if that car had hit him?"

Gert stared at Joe. "What is that to me?" he asked. "I was with you at the church when it happened. How can you accuse me of this?"

"Then it must have been that woman from Immo-Trust," Joe continued. "The one you met with secretly at the market."

"Madame Aut—" Gert bit back the last part of the name. "She returned to Paris the same day. *I* am in charge of this project. And I did nothing to hurt Frank or anyone. That would be against my orders."

Frank touched Joe's shoulder and gestured toward the door. The two brothers walked out into the square.

"I think he's telling the truth," Frank said.

"So who took down the trail sign, and who tried to run you down?" Joe protested. "They've all got alibis . . . from me. I tried to do a timetable yesterday morning. Now, where is it?"

Joe felt in his pants pockets. "Oh, I know. It must be in the jeans I had on yesterday. And I left *them* in the van. I'll be right back."

Joe loped away. Frank took one of the chairs in the square and sat down to think through the mystery.

He had a feeling they were very close to a solution, but what was it?

Joe returned with a look of puzzlement on his face.

"What's up?" Frank asked. "Weren't the jeans there after all?"

"Hmm?" Joe said absently. "Oh—no, they were there. I forgot to bring them."

"Then what?" Frank insisted.

"It's the mileage counter in the van," Joe said. "Yesterday when we left for Peyrane, it was about to hit ten thousand. And this morning, it's at ten thousand and eight."

"Okay," Frank said. "So what?"

"After Kevin dropped us off, he drove all the way to the other side of the valley to do some errands," Joe replied. "Remember? Then he came all the way back to pick us up. So why didn't any of those miles register on the counter?"

"Maybe you misread it," Frank suggested.

"Uh-uh, no way," Joe said. "The only explanation is that he didn't go anywhere. He dropped us at the ocher factory, then sneaked up and changed the trail sign. Then he parked somewhere out of sight, stole a car, and watched for his chance to go after you or me."

"Why us?" Frank demanded. "I don't get it."

A little knot of people came out of the community center. Marina noticed the Hardys and walked over.

"That was so great, this morning," she said. "You really are detectives. I'm so glad Kevin put you on the case."

Frank looked at Joe. "Kevin?" he said. "What do you mean?"

"Well," Marina answered, "I said I wouldn't tell anybody about you, and I didn't. But when Kevin was questioning people about Jean-Claude's bike, I had to tell him. He was really interested, too."

"Yeah, I bet," Joe muttered.

Marina left to rejoin the others. Frank said, "We need to talk to Kevin, right away."

The office was still locked. Frank and Joe walked down the lane to Kevin's cottage. When they knocked on the door, it swung open a crack. They accepted the invitation and went inside. A quick check showed no one in either the upstairs or downstairs rooms. The Hardys started a quick but thorough search.

"Joe, look at this," Frank said after a few minutes. He showed Joe two newspaper clippings. One was a map of Africa, marked to show areas that mined diamonds illegally. The other was an article about the UN conference in Paris. A number of the participants were mentioned. The name of Fenton Hardy was circled in blue ink.

"Impressive," Joe said. "But look at *this!*" He whipped his hand out from behind his back. In it was a black ski mask.

A noise behind them made them spin around. Kevin stood in the doorway. He had a spade in one hand and an old, weathered wooden box in the other. It looked just like the box that had held his ancestor's hoard of raw diamonds.

"I think you need—" Frank began.

With a wild cry, Kevin dropped the box and swung the spade in a shoulder high arc. The edge of the blade glittered as it hurtled toward their necks.

15 The Fréhel Treasure

"Duck!" Frank shouted. He and Joe flung themselves facedown on the floor.

The spade whistled over their heads and crashed against the stone wall. Dust and fragments of rock showered down on them. The spade clattered to the floor.

Frank jumped to his feet. The doorway was empty. Frank and Joe dashed out into the lane. Kevin was running down the path to the parking area. He had the wooden box tucked under one arm.

"Tell Sophie to call the cops," Frank said quickly. "I'll go after him." He sprinted down the lane toward the path. Joe ran in the other direction.

Frank was more than halfway down the path when he heard the whine of the van's engine. Dirt and gravel spurted from under the van's wheels. Kevin accelerated across the parking area toward the track that led outside.

Manu's motorcycle was parked where Frank had left it after his ride. The helmet hung from the handlebar. Was the ignition key still inside?

Frank leaped onto the saddle and grabbed the helmet. His fingers found the key at once. In a series of fluid motions, he donned the helmet, inserted the key, and stood up to kick the starter lever. The motor let out an eager roar. Frank pushed the bike off the kickstand, shoved it in gear, and twisted the throttle full open.

The bike did a wheelie for half the width of the parking area. A rooster tail of dust followed it. Then the front wheel touched down. Frank crouched forward over the fuel tank and sped down the track after Kevin. The van was out of sight, but the layer of dust floating above the track showed that it was not far ahead.

The trail curved around the side of the bluff. Frank picked up speed. On the next turn, he canted the bike over so far that the footrest dug a furrow in the dirt. He backed off the throttle a hair. If he took a spill now, Kevin would be home free. Better to play it safe until he had a clear shot at overtaking the van.

The paved section began just ahead. Frank stood up to soften the jolt, then went back into a crouch and gave it more gas. The powerful motorcycle jumped forward. Around the next curve, the van came in sight. Kevin's lead of fifty yards got shorter with every second. Soon Frank was only a car length behind. He saw Kevin's eyes in the rearview mirror of the van. Was he imagining a look of desperation in them?

A moment later Frank found himself on a straight section of road. A steep bluff ran along one side, like a slanted wall of stone. Along the other was just as steep a drop. Frank moved to the left and opened the throttle full out. His front wheel drew even with Kevin's rear bumper, then with the rear door.

Kevin made a sudden swerve to the left, then to the right. With a scream of tortured tires, the van fishtailed in Frank's direction. Kevin intended to force him off the road, over the cliff!

Frank grabbed the brake handles and squeezed them urgently. The effect made him feel as if he had run straight into a restraining net. His rear wheel lost traction and started to slide sideways. Instantly he turned the handlebars to the left and applied power. The motorcycle straightened up and straightened out.

Frank let out the breath he had been holding. He looked ahead. Kevin had widened his lead again. In a minute or less, he would reach the highway.

Two blue station wagons turned onto the side road and stopped side by side, blocking the way. Red lights revolved on their roofs. The gendarmes! So Joe and Sophie had got through to them in time!

The van's brake lights flashed. Kevin swung to the left, as if he meant to make a swift U-turn. Too swift—the van began to skid sideways. The front wheels went off the edge of the road. For a moment Frank thought the van would topple over. But when the dust cleared, it was still upright. Kevin thrust his door open and put one foot on the ground.

Frank braked to a halt next to him. "Give it up, Kevin," he called. "You can't get away."

One of the police cars sped up. Two uniformed officers jumped out with automatics in their hands.

"It looks like you're right," Kevin said. He placed his hands on the steering wheel, in plain sight, and waited to be arrested.

"Diamonds," Frank said. "Diamonds are the key to the whole case."

He and Joe were in the square at Fréhel. The others from TVI had pulled chairs around to ask questions and get answers.

"You mean the treasure Kevin found?" Siri asked.

"He didn't find a treasure," Joe said. "He only pretended to."

"Why?" Antonio asked.

"There's a major push to stop the illegal traffic in diamonds," Frank explained. "In fact, our dad is at a conference on the subject right now. It's no trick to smuggle diamonds into a country like France. But once they're here, how do you sell them? People want to know where they came from. They want proof they're legitimate."

"That's where Kevin's scheme comes in," Joe said, taking up the story. "He claims to find a two-hundred-year-old hoard of raw diamonds. It's a great story. It hits the news. So when he goes to sell some diamonds, who's going to ask where they came from? They already know. They saw him and his box of diamonds on TV."

"Pretty clever," Welly remarked.

"Brilliant," Frank said. "Nobody knows how many diamonds are in the treasure. As long as he sells them to different people, he can keep doing it for months, even years."

Antonio laughed. "It's like the story about the ever-full pasta bowl," he said. "Only here it's the ever-full box of diamonds!"

"So he made up the whole story?" Libby said. "About his mother's family, and the cottage, and all?"

"We don't know yet," Frank said. "It wouldn't surprise me if his mother's family did come from here. Maybe they even lived in that cottage. But once he was here, he heard the legend of the Fréhel treasure. That must have given him the idea. If there was one legendary treasure in the village, why not another?"

Jean-Claude shook his head. "I couldn't understand. In all the accounts I had never read of this other treasure. Now I see why. Because it didn't exist!"

"Kevin must have been stunned when he heard that we're detectives," Frank continued. "And then to see that an American investigator at the Paris conference has the same last name! He must have been sure that Joe and I had been sent here to spy on him."

"So he decided to scare us off, whatever it took," Joe added. "It's ironic. If he hadn't, I don't know if we would ever have suspected him of anything."

"So, there's no treasure after all?" Libby said wistfully.

"There's still the treasure of the Fréhels," Welly said. "Wherever it may be."

"Perhaps only in our dreams," Marie-Laure said. "And it may not be wise to cling to dreams of riches. It is better to remember the Sieur de Fréhel's own motto: True wealth is found around the family hearth."

Frowning, Frank said, "I remember Jean-Claude quoted that before. What does it mean?"

Marie-Laure seemed surprised by the question. "Why—that life with our family is what is truly important. The word in French is *foyer*. It means 'fireplace,' but it also means the family home."

Frank felt a bubble of excitement growing in his mind. "Are you saying that your ancestor, the guy who hid the treasure, made a point of telling his family that they would find wealth around the fireplace? And none of them bothered to search there?"

Frank looked around the circle of stunned faces.

"Would a couple of you go get a long ladder?" he asked.

From below, the fireplace in the great hall of the chateau looked big. Up close, it was enormous. When Frank stepped off the ladder, he automatically stooped, but it was needless. The top arch of the masonry was at least a foot taller than he. He moved to one side to let Joe, Marie-Laure, and Jean-Claude join him.

"What did they burn in this thing?" Joe wondered. "Whole tree trunks?"

"In fact, yes," Marie-Laure told him. "It was all they had for heat."

Frank scanned the walls of the fireplace. The smoke-darkened stones looked as solid as, well, as rock. He took a hammer from his belt and began tapping on the stones.

Ten minutes later he stopped. "I don't hear anything that sounds hollow," he said. "Maybe our theory is wrong."

The spectators in the room below were beginning to look restless. Too bad, Frank thought. This wasn't for their amusement.

Jean-Claude was fiddling with the rusty iron hooks that protruded from the fireplace walls. "Hey," he suddenly said. "This one turns."

The three others joined him. He was right. With a sound like fingernails on a blackboard, the hook

148

turned a quarter turn counterclockwise. Frank was sure he heard a click at the end.

"Help me," he said. He wedged his fingertips in a crack between the stones. "Pull!"

Just when Frank was beginning to think they were wasting their energy, the entire side wall of the fireplace started to swing outward.

Those down below shouted with excitement. Frank, Joe, and the two Fréhels held their collective breath.

Jean-Claude had a flashlight. He shone it into the growing gap. "A skull!" he gasped. "It's looking straight at me!" The flashlight fell from his fingers.

Marie-Laure scooped up the flashlight and aimed it into the dark niche. Frank looked over her shoulder and caught his breath.

Propped against the far wall of the tiny compartment was the form of a man. White bones gleamed amid tatters of ancient cloth. The skeleton leaned sideways onto a wooden chest. One side of the chest had rotted away. A river of sparkling jewels cascaded from the chest to the rough stone floor.

"The Sieur de Fréhel's treasure," Marie-Laure whispered. "We've found it!"

Frank noticed a gold ring on the floor. He picked it up. A coat of arms was engraved on its face. He could just make out the last word of the motto underneath. It was *foyer*.

149

"I think we just found the Sieur de Fréhel, too," Frank said solemnly.

Jean-Claude met his eyes. "I don't understand," he said. "The bandits confessed that they threw his body from the battlements. It is in the official court records. How did it come to be here, in this secret place, next to his treasure?"

Frank looked at the skull. In the wavering light of the flash, it seemed to look back at him.

"I don't know," Frank said. "Maybe there are some mysteries that we shouldn't expect to solve."

Todd Strasser's
AGAINST THE ODDS™

Shark Bite
The sailboat is sinking, and Ian just saw the biggest shark of his life.

Grizzly Attack
They're trapped in the Alaskan wilderness with no way out.

Buzzard's Feast
Danger in the desert!

Gator Prey
They know the gators are coming for them...it's only a matter of time.

Published by Simon & Schuster   2023-01

BILL WALLACE

Award-winning author Bill Wallace brings you fun-filled
animal stories full of humor and exciting adventures.

Published by Simon & Schuster   648-33/01

The Fascinating Story of One of the World's Most Celebrated Naturalists

Celebrating 40 years with the wild chimpanzees

MY LIFE with the CHIMPANZEES

by JANE GOODALL

From the time she was girl, Jane Goodall dreamed of a life spent working with animals. Finally, when she was twenty-six years old, she ventured into the forests of Africa to observe chimpanzees in the wild. On her expeditions she braved the dangers of the jungle and survived encounters with leopards and lions in the African bush. And she got to know an amazing group of wild chimpanzees—intelligent animals whose lives bear a surprising resemblance to our own.

Illustrated with photographs

A Byron Preiss Visual Publications, Inc. Book

Published by Simon & Schuster

2403-0